Y0-EDQ-809

The Night of the Falcon

The Night of the Falcon

JAMES OXFORD

ST. MARTIN'S PRESS ◆ NEW YORK

Design by Laura Hammond

10 9 8 7 6 5 4 3 2 1

First Edition

ISBN 0-312-57302-2

T he wet cold winds of late September came sweeping southeast down the slopes of the towering Alps. From the wind-chopped waters of Lake Locarno in the north as far south as Bologna, the old men sniffed at the damp air and nodded knowingly as they waited for the rains soon to follow.

Spread across the upper calf of the Italian boot from the Adriatic on the east to the Ligurian Sea on the west, Feldmarshal Albrecht Kesselring's twenty-five German divisions grudgingly gave up yards and then miles as they were pushed out of the Gothic Line they had been ordered by the Führer himself to hold or die. The combined British and American forces under General Harold Alexander pressed slowly northward, fighting for each shell-pocked foot of ground, probing, looking for the soft spot that would crack the German front and let them go racing up the thick thigh of Italy for the passes through the Alps into Austria.

The heavy dark clouds gathered along the mountain wall and moved south, and the rains began in mid-October. Kesselring's Waffen SS divisions and paratroopers, together with two divisions of Fascist Italian troops, fell back through the hills and rivers towards the south valley of the Po. Torrential rains turned the roads and countryside into quagmires of mud, stopping the Allied attack more effectively than the German guns. The rains gave the remnants of the

German Army in Italy seven more months of life.

But if a one-word message radioed out of a small town nearly three hundred miles from the embattled front was accurate, fighting could last much longer.

The rains that swept the length of Italy day after day sent rivulets of water pouring over the cobblestoned streets of Aosta, nestled in a valley between the Garian and Pennine Alps, just a few miles from the French frontier on the west and the Swiss border to the north.

The drumming beat of the rain muffled the slight sounds Giovanni Bertolli made as he slipped through the small side door of the old house at the edge of Aosta. It had once been the home of the Maccelli family, but they now lived with relatives and the house was shared by a Wehrmacht major and a Waffen SS captain.

The houses to either side also were officer quarters, and a pair of sodden German troopers were supposed to be making steady guard patrols around the three buildings. But both guards stood huddled in the doorway of one of the other houses, waiting for a break in the downpour.

His rage and his pride had been boiling for more than a month since the terrible afternoon when Lucetta, his Lucetta, had laughed at him and walked away. She had stopped, pirouetted so that her skirts flared to display the new black silk stockings. Then, still laughing, she had turned the corner out of his life.

Her words burned in his brain.

"You're not even a man," she taunted, "just a poor useless *paisano*. A nothing. What can you give me? Nothing. At least Karl is generous, and he's more of a man than you."

Giovanni was soaked, his old shoes making sloshing noises as he eased around a corner and listened for sounds in the house. As he stood and listened, he pushed the wet shoes from his bare feet. The house was silent, only the incessant pounding of the rain echoing off the roof and windows. The Wehrmacht major occupied the sleeping room on the first floor. Waffen SS Captain Karl Mueller had the second floor. They must be up there.

He edged along the wall towards the narrow stairwell, an eighteen-year-old boy torn by love, hate and fright. The thin, razor-edged hunting knife in its worn sheath pressed against his groin where it was tucked inside his waistband. Giovanni had turned eighteen last week, and now he was a man, a man whose honor was besmirched so badly that only blood could wash away the stain. When this was over, he would take to the hills, join one of the many anti-Fascist guerrilla groups scattered throughout northern Italy. They still fought both the Germans and Fascist Italians, even though Rome had been liberated by Allied forces four months earlier. Kesselring had retreated northward, finally taking a stand again behind the Gothic Line and drawing with him the Fascist groups. Mussolini was in hiding at Lake Garda, after being rescued by German paratroops from exile in the south.

The door to the major's room was partially ajar, and Giovanni heard the reassuring sounds of snoring as he darted past the door to the foot of the stairs. Step by step he inched his way upwards, shuddering at each slight creak of the old wooden stairs. At the upper landing he stopped and listened again. He could hear the faint sounds of breathing coming from the open door of the captain's room. He had been in the house several times earlier as part of a town work force ordered to help German troops get settled into Aosta. The little town had been a German Army headquarters for the northwestern regions of Italy for more than two years.

He slipped the knife from its sheath and held it, palm-up, as he slipped inside the door. It was pitch-black in the room, and here, on the upper floor of the old house, the hard-driven rain rattled the slates of the roof, effectively overriding all but the loudest noises he might make. The boy silently and hatefully prayed that the bed was still in the same position it had been in when he had helped carry things into the room six months ago, the day the Waffen SS officer had moved in.

The room was small, and it would be difficult to change the position of the furniture. For the past month he had tormented himself with mental images of his Lucetta lying in that bed, legs thrown wide to receive the pumping, moving German officer sprawled over her soft moist body. His eyes, now adjusting to the dark, made out the two sleeping forms in the bed against the far wall, just a few steps distant. The larger body lay under the covers at the left side of the bed, nearest to the boy. Inch by inch he moved closer to the bed until he stood looking down in the shadowy dim light at the close-cropped blond head of the German. He was lying on his back, one arm thrown over the body of the girl who lay on her side next to him, her soft behind pressed for warmth against his bared thigh.

Until that instant, he had never really believed the terrible images his mind had conjured. Now it was reality, and all of the hatred of a passionate Italian male welled up across his eyes like a blood-red curtain. His hand rolled over, and with one quick hard slashing movement he cut into the bared throat of the German, cutting so deeply he felt the blade strike the bones at the back of the neck. Mueller's body convulsed and heaved once as a fountain of blood arched from his severed throat. His death cry was only a gurgling muted sound.

The spurting blood drenched the front of Giovanni's jacket and struck the side of his face as he leaned over the body of the German. Lucetta had stirred restlessly at the movement of Mueller's body but had not turned. The boy whipped the covers from her body. She rolled onto her back and opened her eyes wide. At the moment the knife came plunging down to bury itself just below the dark circle of her

4

left nipple, she screamed. Then the blade sliced into the heart wall, and she was dead.

Giovanni paused a second to look at the dead lovers and then heaved and vomited over their bloodstained bodies. Trying to contain his own churning stomach, he raced for the door and thudded barefooted down the stairs.

The scream had awakened the Wehrmacht major. He was standing at the foot of the steps, Luger in hand, as the hurtling figure of the boy came down. He had time to get off a single shot before Bertolli's body hit him, knocking him from his feet and slamming his head against the doorjamb. The two lay there for several seconds, the major unconscious, the boy just beginning to feel the excruciating pain starting in his gut where the shot had penetrated.

Slowly he rolled over onto his knees and then got to his feet, both hands clutching at his belly. Lurching in the dark, he staggered towards the back door, wanting only to get away from the house and from the terrible pain lancing his body.

Still barefooted and doubled over, he plunged out of the rear door into the driving rain as one of the two Wehrmacht guards came running around the far side of the house, machine pistol at the ready.

"*Halten sie,*" the soldier cried.

Now consumed by pain, Giovanni never even heard the challenge. His shoulder smashed into the outer wall as he took two staggering steps towards the sentry. The Schmeisser machine pistol erupted, and the boy was slammed back into the mud of the alley, dead before his head splashed into the cold gurgling stream of water pouring down the gutter.

The other sentry raced around the corner of the building, and the two moved cautiously in the dark rain-swept night to where Giovanni lay. The man who had killed him nudged the prone body with his foot and looked up in satisfaction. Up the block both sentries heard the pounding of feet as the curfew patrol came streaming down the street towards the sound of the shots.

Lights began glimmering in the rain as other German officers in the nearby houses were aroused from their sleep and hastily threw on clothes and seized firearms to defend themselves against possible attack.

Inside the Maccelli house, the Wehrmacht major groaned and then sat up. He rubbed the swelling at the back of his head, and then stood up and found the switch to the dim hall light. He picked up his pistol. Blood, that had dripped from the wound in Giovanni's belly and from his jacket, trailed down the stairs and around the corner towards the back door. With a muffled oath, the major painfully pounded up the stairs, calling out to the Waffen SS captain.

Getting no response, he reached inside the darkened door of Mueller's room and found the light switch. One look at the crimson bodies on the bed and the Wehrmacht major turned and raced down the stairs for the rear door. He came charging out of the door into the rain and was almost shot by the startled soldiers standing over Giovanni's body.

Five minutes later, the field telephone rang in the Savoldi Castle, perched high on a hillside above Aosta and now the headquarters for Alpengruppe Zwei (II), commanded by General Wilhelm Meirhausser. The centuries-old crenellated building, known locally as Vulcano Castle, was both command post and residence for not only Meirhausser but also for senior Alpengruppe Gestapo Major Conrad Koppfman.

The night duty NCO listened briefly, and then replaced the phone and ran down a long dark corridor of the building to the rear suite of rooms occupied by Koppfman. The *feldwebel* pounded on the door and, without waiting for an answer, walked into the room.

Koppfman was just reaching for the light beside his bed.

He sat up, tousle-headed, and glared at the soldier.

"Why are you disturbing me at this hour of the night?" he snarled at the rigid figure of the NCO standing at the foot of the bed.

"Begging the major's pardon," the German sergeant shouted, his right arm snapping up and out in the Nazi salute, "but there has been a murder in the village. A German officer, Herr Major."

Koppfman's eyes widened, and he threw back the covers and swung his feet to the floor.

"Tell them I'll be down there in ten minutes," he said, reaching for his uniform. "Have a staff car waiting at the door for me." He paused and listened to the pounding sounds of the rain beating against the windowpanes. He shivered in the cold damp old room and began pulling on his clothing. *"Grosse Gott,"* he muttered as he pulled on black uniform pants and boots, "why does everything have to happen in shitty weather?" He looked at his watch. It was just after three in the morning.

An hour later, he strode back into the cold stone main hall of Vulcano Castle, shaking the rain from his drenched cap and slipping out of his sodden topcoat.

The four night-duty men at the desks in the hall snapped to attention as he entered. "Find Weber, the general's orderly," Koppfman snapped at the NCO. "Tell him to discreetly but urgently awaken the general. It is a matter of emergency."

"Zu befehl, Herr Major."

At the door to Meirhausser's room, the sleepy orderly looked at his watch and nodded to himself. Frau Savoldi would be in her own bed at this hour. He knocked sharply on the door.

◆　　◆　　◆

The incessant knocking finally penetrated the sleep of the dark-haired Italian girl. She sat up in bed, the covers

7

falling below her heavy hard-nippled breasts. The man in the bed beside her continued sleeping, his occasional snores giving off slight sounds and the heavy sour smell of too much cognac.

"Who is it?" she called out in Italian.

"Corporal McKenzie, ma'am," a man's voice responded in English. "Will you please ask the captain to come to the door? It's most urgent."

"*Un momento,*" she called out and switched to English. "I'll try."

She turned and gently rocked the sleeping man's shoulder. He didn't move. She shook him more vigorously.

"Eduardo, Eduardo," she called out, "wake up, *carissimo,* there's one of your men at the door."

Canadian S.O.E. intelligence officer and field agent, Captain Ed Kimball tried to pull the covers over his head and moaned.

The girl grinned at him and shook even harder. He had picked her up four nights ago in a bar, and since then they had spent every night and part of each day locked in sweaty lovemaking in her bed. But he had proved to be not only a good lover but a generous one. Her pile of lira grew with each twenty-four hours. If only he hadn't drunk so much, she would have been well pleased, both physically and financially.

But Kimball had been slightly drunk when he met her and had gotten progressively drunker with each passing day and night.

She put her mouth at his ear and hissed. "Eduardo, wake up, you drunken idiot. Someone's at the door."

The only response was another attempt to burrow deeper into the covers.

"Please hurry, miss," the soldier standing outside the door called.

"I'm trying," she called back. "Wait a minute."

Sunlight was filtering through the drawn drapes, and the fresh clean smell of the sea fought a losing battle against the stale alcoholic breath of the sleeping man.

Reaching beneath the covers, the girl groped for Kimball's crotch.

Almost immediately he began to harden. A sleepy smile came over his face, and he rolled onto his back, eyes still closed. His arm groped for the girl, trying to pull her atop him.

Laughingly, she slipped out of his grasp and pulled the covers off his long muscular form, the jagged vivid scar of a knife pulsing on his chest and the lesser scars of bullet wounds pocking his strong thighs.

Even in southern Bari, far to the south of the Alps and crowding the waters of the Adriatic, the early fall weather chilled the air.

The girl jumped from the bed, throwing on a robe, and dashed to the window beside the bed. She whipped open the drapes and spread the double panes wide. A blast of cold sea air bathed Kimball's nude form.

With a gasp he sat up in bed and stared red-eyed around the room.

"Wha' the hell," he mumbled as he tried to find the covers. His head throbbed miserably. He jerked around and winced as he saw the girl grinning at him from the wide-open windows. "Shut those goddamn windows, woman!" he yelled. "You lost your fucking mind?" He grasped at his head and moaned.

The whore came back and sat on the edge of the bed beside him.

"Eduardo, there is one of your soldiers at the door. He wants to talk to you. Right now. Get up and see him." She handed him his uniform trousers draped on a chair beside the bed.

Kimball stared at her drunkenly for a couple of mo-

9

ments until her words finally penetrated. He lifted his aching head and called out, "Who's there?"

"Me, sir, McKenzie," came the reply. "Colonel Bancroft wants you in his office immediately, sir. Sorry about that."

"Fuck Colonel Bancroft," Kimball called back. "Get lost, McKenzie."

"Afraid I can't do that, sir," the corporal replied. "The colonel said it is most urgent. Some sort of a flap up. I'm to bring you to his office without fail."

Kimball blinked drunkenly and reached down beside the bed, his hand groping for the nearly empty bottle of cognac. He pulled out the loose cork and let a stream of the fiery cheap brandy pour down his throat. A violent fit of coughing seized him, and the girl pounded him on the back.

"Please, Eduardo," she pleaded, "get up. Talk to your man."

The coughing stopped, and Kimball's eyes widened as the liquor hit his stomach. He shook his head and then clumsily climbed into the trousers the girl was holding for him.

He lurched to the door and cracked it open.

The noncom snapped to a salute and tried to keep from grinning at the sight of the disheveled officer.

"Colonel Bancroft's compliments, sir," he said, "and will you please report to him at once? I have a jeep outside."

Kimball gazed half-drunkenly at the soldier. "You're not handing me a line, are you, McKenzie?"

"No, sir. God's word on it, Captain. The colonel is really sizzling."

"OK, OK," the intelligence officer mumbled, "be down in a few minutes. Wait for me in the jeep."

"Please make it snappy, Captain," McKenzie said. "The colonel has just about turned Bari upside down trying to find you."

Kimball nodded and shut the door. He turned and went back towards the bed. The girl had closed the windows and was back under the covers.

The Canadian grinned at her and staggered to her side of the bed, unzipping his pants. He sat down and reached for her breasts. The girl pulled away. "No, Eduardo, as much as I'd like it. You must go. Otherwise, we will both be in trouble. I will be here waiting for you when you are through with *Signore Colonnello.*"

Disgustedly, Kimball pulled back and went to the other side of the bed to find the rest of his uniform. For nearly three weeks, ever since returning from his last fucked-up mission, the tall sandy-haired rancher's son from Edmonton had steadily and doggedly been getting drunk and trying to stay that way to wipe out, at least temporarily, the memories of that last job.

Fumbling awkwardly with buttons and belt, at last he was dressed. He bent down beside the bed and groaned as his head protested. He felt under the bed until he found a full bottle of liquor and then slowly got to his feet, his head throbbing. He blinked to clear the pain and then smiled drunkenly at the girl.

"Gotta go," he said. "Keep it warm for me, baby. I'll be back." He turned towards the door.

"Eduardo," the girl said softly, "I would be able to wait more patiently if I could buy a new dress."

Kimball nodded and fished in his pants pocket. "Almost forgot. Sorry." He pulled out a loose wad of banknotes and dropped half of them on the bureau at the side of the room.

Waving at the girl, he made his painful way down the hall to the waiting jeep. He winced as he stepped out into the bright sunlight. The rain clouds that had engulfed the seaport of Bari for the past three days and which had poured rain into the city were gone, and now the clean rain-washed buildings shone in the bright early-morning light. In the distance, the blue of the Adriatic shimmered with dancing whitecaps and sparkling sun.

Kimball climbed heavily into the waiting jeep.

◆　　◆　　◆

Standing in the town square in Aosta, Gestapo Major Conrad Koppfman glanced at his watch. It was exactly nine o'clock. He looked up at the Waffen SS lieutenant standing a few feet away and nodded. The rains were gone, at least for a few hours, and bright sun lighted the mountain town.

Despite the sun and the unexpected warmth of the fall day, every window facing the square was closed and shuttered. Only German soldiers and officials were on the streets, even the Italian Fascists staying indoors or away from town. The sole Italian civilians present among Aosta's two thousand residents were the twenty men, ranging in ages from sixteen to seventy-two, tied to stakes in the middle of the square. At Koppfman's nod, the Waffen SS officer shouted a single-word command.

The two heavy machine guns, set up on tripods thirty feet in front of the trussed hostages, opened automatic fire, the Waffen gunners holding their fingers on the triggers and sweeping left and right across the line of victims. All twenty were dead in ten seconds. The firing stopped, and absolute silence gripped not only the square but the entire town as the sound of the firing echoed off the surrounding hills and through the narrow winding streets.

The Waffen officer walked slowly down the line of slumped tied figures. He paused at each and placed his pistol at the back of a head and fired. He reloaded and continued until he reached the end of the line.

The machine guns had been knocked down and were already loaded back into their vehicles. The Waffen gun crews stood at attention beside the weapons carrier. The lieutenant nodded, and the noncom in charge muttered a short command. The executioners swung into the truck and drove off. The officer walked to Koppfman's staff car where the Gestapo officer waited for him. He climbed in, and the vehicle departed.

Only the dead were left, bleeding and slumped at the base of the stakes driven into the rain-softened dirt of the town square.

Long minutes passed after the last of the German vehicles had departed. Then they came, old men, black-garbed women with shawls over their heads, walking slowly into the square. Muted and muffled sobs broke the sound of shuffling feet. From a side street, a long farm cart, its bed already spread with blankets, creaked into the square behind an ancient horse.

Quietly, gently and lovingly, tears silently streaming down their faces, they untied each body and carefully laid it on the blanket-covered floor of the cart. When all twenty had been loaded, the cart, followed by the still silent and grieving small crowd, moved around the square and came to a halt in front of the village church. The priest was waiting. When the cart stopped, he climbed into the back, ignoring the seeping blood that stained the hem of his vestments. He tried unsuccessfully to stem his own tears as he slowly moved from one body to another, administering extreme unction. When he had given all twenty final rites, he climbed laboriously from the cart and sank to his knees on the steps of the church, facing the unseen altar within.

As if on cue, as the entire crowd knelt with him, the big bell in the church tower began its slow tolling of twenty-one notes, for the twenty hostages and for Giovanni Bertolli.

When the priest completed reciting the prayers for the dead, he rose and walked slowly into the church. The cart moved off, followed by its growing entourage, to stop at twenty houses where the bullet-torn bodies were carried in to be cleaned and prepared for burial.

Now the wails of grief drifted out into the morning and

13

floated agonizingly among the walls of the narrow streets. They were unheard in Vulcano Castle as Koppfman climbed out of his car and went in to confer with General Wilhelm Meirhausser.

◆ ◆ ◆

At forty-three, "Willi" Meirhausser was every Aryan German's image of what a Prussian Wehrmacht officer should be. Tall, blond and handsome, his hair was carefully swept back in waves from his high forehead. His immaculate uniform was tailored to the perfection of his muscular body, and the Knight's Cross that he had won early in the war in Poland gleamed at his throat. The medal and a slight limp were his rewards from a grateful Führer, together with what then appeared to be a dream assignment two years ago, command of the northern Italian Alpengruppe.

Hitler had never trusted Mussolini and had a sneering disdain for the abilities of Italian war power. He became convinced of this in the mass surrenders of Italian troops in North Africa, leaving Rommel and the Afrika Corps to attempt to stand in the face of massive Allied attacks. It was at this point, long before the invasion of Sicily, that German manpower and German military strategists began moving into Italy. Even more than Churchill, Hitler and the German High Command were conscious of the "soft underbelly of Europe." If Africa fell, it was only a question of time and location before the Allies crossed the Mediterranean. Hitler had no intention of leaving the back door to Austria and Germany open to invaders.

Meirhausser got the northern Italian assignment, and within months Africa fell, Sicily was invaded and the Italian government surrendered. Only a few thousand Fascist troops remained loyal to the exiled Mussolini. Italy was open to full invasion from boot heel to boot top and, with it, possible Allied excursions into the Balkans.

Despite the terrible need for more troops at the crumbling Russian front, the Germans poured divisions into Italy. The deadly battles of Cassino, Anzio and, finally, north of Rome, fell totally upon German soldiers of the Third Reich.

Willi Meirhausser was given two missions, one more important and secret than the other.

Alpengruppe II had the primary mission of ultimately stopping dead in its tracks any Allied assault that might possibly break through the several southern lines of defense established by the Germans. Anzio cracked the Mussolini Line, and Rome fell. Now British General Alexander on the right and American General Mark Clark on the left were smashing slowly through the Gothic Line. German troops were falling back to the Po River. Should the Po be breached, then the ancient corridors of the Brenner Pass leading into Austria and, subsequently, Bavaria would be open to the Allies.

The set piece of Hitler's Alpine defense was to be *Festung Bergskrieg*—the Mountain War Fortress—dug deeply into the Trentino Alto Adige, the north-to-south Alpine range bordering the Brenner route on the west and, in the Dolomites, flanking the route on the east. This was ultra-secret Project Guardian, and its construction and completion were Willi Meirhausser's prime missions. Work on the inter-locked series of underground forts and strong points had already begun, although Allied air raids not only postponed its start but hampered German efforts to move slave labor and material for the work.

It was because of its highly secret nature that Alpengruppe II headquarters had been established in Aosta, more than 150 miles from the actual construction sites. Any military headquarters of size generates a heavy flow of traffic and eventually becomes known to the enemy. The German High Command wanted no headquarters in the vicinity of Project Guardian, to lessen chances of a leak.

When Meirhausser first arrived in Aosta, it had taken

no more than a few hours to settle on the Savoldi Castle as the most desirable site for a headquarters.

Built in the thirteenth century, the sprawling stone structure had been in the Savoldi family since the first block was laid. Over the hundreds of years, it had been added to and undermined by deep storerooms and even escape tunnels for the castle's occupants, on the unlikely chance that the battlements might be overrun by an attacking force.

The last male heir in the line, Count Milo Savoldi, left his mountain home for the sea, becoming an Italian naval officer.

The war was less than a year old when Savoldi died off the coast of North Africa in a one-sided battle between his light destroyer and a heavy British cruiser.

When Meirhausser arrived in Aosta, Vulcano Castle was occupied only by Savoldi's stunningly beautiful widow Riva and a handful of servants. There were no children of the marriage just two years before the start of the war. Struck both by her beauty and grace, the handsome and chivalrous Meirhausser insisted that she remain in the castle and, in essence, play the unwanted role of hostess to the high-ranking German officers who would be stationed there or passing through. And, in particular, to look elegant and lovely in that role on the arm of the dashing Willi Meirhausser.

◆　◆　◆

Koppfman was ushered into Meirhausser's office. The door closed behind him as he threw the Wehrmacht general a Nazi salute.

Meirhausser ignored the outstretched arm. "Will you please be so kind, Major, as to tell me what the hell is going on around here?" he growled.

With Gestapo-born insolence, Koppfman slouched into a chair across from the general without being invited to sit.

"We have a problem, Herr General," Koppfman said, "and I have already started taking care of it."

"That stupid Karl Mueller?" Meirhausser asked.

"That stupid thing, as you call it," the other man replied, "could be just the kind of incident to trigger off a new wave of partisan attacks. And at this point that's the last thing we can afford."

The general tilted back in his chair and surveyed the Gestapo officer. "You mean to tell me that a dumb Heidelberger getting himself killed by some love-crazy Italian kid is a serious incident?"

"Look, Herr General," Koppfman said, leaning forward in his chair to emphasize his point, "we have had almost eight months of reasonable quiet around here. We hit the partisan groups hard early this year, and they're all but wiped out. Three months ago, no Italian, no matter how much he hated a German for taking his woman, would have dared to try an attack, and certainly not on a Waffen SS officer.

"But it happened, and it's just the kind of incident to light these stupid peasants once again. We have effectively cut down almost every partisan group from the French border to Yugoslavia. With Kesselring already giving ground on the Gothic, you cannot afford to have a single leak at this point in Project Guardian."

Meirhausser stared at the map of northern Italy on the wall beside his desk. He rubbed his chin thoughtfully.

"You're probably right, Koppfman," he said; "this could mean trouble. I'll issue orders this morning for no further fraternization with any Italians, especially women. If they get horny, let them use the whorehouse. Is that still secure?"

Koppfman nodded. "Every woman in it is non-Italian, and we have enough wire and guards around it twenty-four hours a day that nobody other than German troops with proper passes can get in. None of the whores can so much as step foot outside the wire."

"All right," the general said, "the orders go out immediately. What else?"

"I'm starting this morning," the Gestapo officer said, "as if I had never uncovered any of the traitor groups. I've gotten word out to every one of my informers to feed me immediately with the slightest hint of partisan activity. And for openers, I've given these pigs in Aosta something to remember the next time anyone of them thinks about attacking a German."

Meirhausser's eyebrows raised questioningly.

"We executed twenty of their animal-like males in the town square this morning, and if there's so much as a word of complaint about it, I'll kill another twenty."

Meirhausser stared bleakly at the Gestapo officer and sighed. "I suppose it's necessary, but this is a rotten way for a soldier to fight, shooting unarmed civilians tied to stakes."

Koppfman rose and stood in front of the desk, looking down at the Wehrmacht general. "Look, Herr General, this is not the Middle Ages. Wars are not fought today by knights in shining armor going forth to do battle in single combat. We are fighting for the very future of the Third Reich and for all Germans against enemies on every side. In this war, there are no noncombatants. Either they are with us, or they are our enemies. Now, if you'll excuse me, I have work to do. Heil Hitler."

Koppfman walked out of the room.

Meirhausser sat idly at his desk for a moment and then called his adjutant into the room and gave the new nonfraternization orders. Then he rose and walked out of the office and up the worn marble steps of the castle to the second floor. The long corridors, dark with their tiny wall bulbs of low wattage, made the building seem cold and dank, even in midsummer. Now, with fall in the making and winter not far away, Meirhausser shivered slightly as he made his way down the dim passageway. At the door to Riva Savoldi's room, he knocked lightly.

"Come," her voice called.

He walked into her private sitting room. Almost immediately, the sight of the raven-haired slim Italian beauty brought a smile to his lips.

She was sitting at an *armoire écritoire,* notepaper in front of her, pen in hand. At his entrance she turned, and her face lighted with a smile.

"Willi, how nice. What brings you up here at this hour of the morning? I should think you would be working hard at your desk, making all those great plans that generals always make." She raised her hand to him.

He stopped in front of her and bowed with just the barest clicking of his heels. He took her hand and pressed it lightly to his lips.

"How beautiful you look this morning, my darling," he said.

"And how gallant you are this morning," she smiled wickedly. "A raving sex maniac last night and now a gallant chevalier this morning."

Meirhausser grinned and sat down on the couch across from her.

"May I return the compliment," he said, "by saying you are a delicious whore in the dark and the most courtly and beautiful gentlewoman by day that I have ever known."

Riva wrinkled her nose. "Enough of flattery. What brings you here so early, Willi?"

The officer pulled out a case and extracted a cigarette. Lighting it, he drew deeply and then leaned back on the couch.

"There was a bit of trouble in town last night, Riva," he said. "Some crazy kid sneaked into a house and cut Karl Mueller's throat as he lay sleeping."

Riva's hand went to her mouth. "How awful," she exclaimed. "Whatever reason did the boy have?"

"It would appear that he caught Karl asleep in bed with his girl friend. He killed her, too. Luckily, Karl's fellow officer in the other bedroom heard the commotion and managed to shoot the assassin. The sentries finished him off."

"Who was the boy?" she asked.

Meirhausser pulled a notebook from his jacket and consulted it briefly. "Some kid named Giovanni Bertolli."

Inwardly Riva shuddered and felt the bile rising in her throat. The Bertolli family had been in Aosta almost as long as the Savoldis, and for generations both men and women of the Bertolli family had worked at many tasks in the big castle. They were part of the castle family, as were so many of the families in the town.

"In any case, my dear one," the German continued, "this may have sparked some new partisan troubles. Koppfman is going to crack down hard once again. I've issued orders for no German troops to fraternize in any way with Italian women."

Riva stared at him coldly. "And that, Herr General, includes me, of course."

"*Liebchen, liebchen,*" Meirhausser cried, leaping to his feet and pulling Riva's head to his chest, "for God's sake, you know better than that. This has nothing to do with us."

He hugged her tighter.

Riva Savoldi pulled away and turned her head. "I am an Italian woman, Willi. Are you not afraid that I, too, will lead to trouble?"

"You talk like a silly idiot," Meirhausser said with exasperation. "The only thing I'm afraid of is that you might come to some harm. That's the reason for my visit. I must ask you to remain inside the grounds for a few days until this has quieted down. I'm quite sure that Koppfman will have it in hand very soon."

"I'm sure you're right, Willi. The major is most efficient," she said coolly. "When does this house arrest begin?"

Meirhausser rolled his eyes to the ceiling. "Riva, Riva," he cried. "It's not house arrest. This is for your own safety, my darling. And it begins right now."

She rose and went over to him, a smile on her face, her fingers idly twisting a button on his uniform.

"Oh, Willi, not today, please. This is the day I get my last fitting for the gown that Signora Quaremba is making for me. Please, Willi, just a short trip."

Meirhausser shook his head. "Why not have her bring it here to the castle?" he said. "She can finish the fitting here."

"You men are all so ignorant of what women do," she said, putting her arms around his neck and pulling him down. "She can't bring it here because it's on a clothes form, made especially for me. Please, my darling. This is very important. You know that we're less than a week from the party, and I must have the gown. If you're worried about me, then send some of your men with me. I won't be more than a half hour." She pulled his head down and kissed him wetly. "Please, Willi."

The tall German officer smiled down at her. "Very well, just this one last time," he agreed. "But you go down in my car with a squad of men. No one else will be allowed in the shop while you're in there, understood?"

"Oh, thank you, Willi, I knew you would understand."

Meirhausser turned to leave. "Somehow, my darling, you always seem to have your way," he said as he reached the door.

Again that impish smile crossed her lips. "I have my way by day, and you have your way by night."

Meirhausser flushed, laughed and walked out of the room.

An hour later, with six armed Wehrmacht soldiers crowded into the general's big armor-plated limousine, Riva arrived at the little house that was also the dressmaking shop.

"*Bitte,* Frau Savoldi," the sergeant in charge of the detail turned in the front seat to speak. "Please remain in the car until we have checked out the house and posted guards. Herr General's orders."

Riva sighed and made a face. "Oh, very well."

Four of the soldiers entered the little house, while the other two stood at either side of the vehicle, automatic weapons at ready. The street was deserted.

In a few minutes the sergeant returned. "You may enter now."

She got out and walked past the two men guarding the front door. Another soldier was inside, and she assumed the remainder would be at the back and sides of the little house.

The elderly Italian woman was waiting for her, a smile on her face.

"Ah, Signora Savoldi, just in time. We make the last fitting this morning. You will come, please," she beckoned into the little room beyond. As the two women moved to the door, the soldier was right behind them.

Riva turned and placed a hand firmly on his chest. "No men allowed," she said in German. "This is a ladies' room."

"But Frau Savoldi," he protested, "I have orders to keep you under close guard."

Riva gestured towards the inner room.

"Go in there now," she ordered the man, "and look around for hidden spies. There is no other door. When you are sure it's quite empty, then you come out and wait right here. Now go." She shoved him gently toward the door.

The young Wehrmacht trooper blushed and went gingerly into the other room. He returned almost immediately.

"It is safe," he said firmly. "I will stand guard at this door."

Riva smiled at him and followed the other woman into the room, closing the door behind her. Instantly, she reached into her bodice and extracted a small slip of paper. "This must be sent immediately," she said.

The other woman nodded and stuffed the slip between her own ample breasts. "We shall try. You have heard of the trouble?" she asked as she fussed with the gown on the

22

tailor's dummy in the center of the room.

"You mean about the Bertolli boy? I am sick," Riva said.

The woman looked up at her quickly. "And what about the others?" she demanded.

"What others?" Riva asked.

"The twenty men, no, not men, some just children, that they shot to death this morning in the square. Are they not to be mourned also?"

Riva sank into a nearby chair and bowed her head. She crossed herself and let the tears come. "Oh, sweet Mother of God, have mercy on their souls," she wailed. "I didn't know."

The dressmaker came and put a hand on her shoulder. "Compose yourself, signorina; they are gone and you have work to do. There will be a time for grieving later, when these animals have been killed. Now, dry your eyes and put on the gown."

Riva, again in control of herself, left the shop twenty minutes later and was driven back to the castle.

By midafternoon, a few of Aosta's residents were out on necessary errands. The twenty stakes, with pools of drying blood at the base of each, remained mute reminders in the square.

The dressmaker made her way down the street, market basket on her arm. At the baker's shop, she waited until she was the only customer. Then she slipped the note to the man with the instructions that it must be sent immediately.

As he placed the slip in his pocket, his face was gray and drawn. "It is very dangerous," he said. "The Gestapo are everywhere since last night."

"I know," she said, "but if it wasn't important, the signora would not risk our lives. It must go out."

The baker was one of four men who still maintained a small but relatively inactive partisan unit in the town. Their principal mission was to transmit messages from the small hand-cranked generator-driven radio hidden in a barn.

It was coming up on ten-fifteen that night when the four were assembled in the barn, a single shaded candle for light. One of the four sat turning the generator handset while the operator held his hand poised over the key, eyes on his watch for the prescribed moment for transmission. The other two stood guard inside the door, pistols in hand.

The sweep hand on the watch came around, and the radio operator nodded, and the generator man cranked faster.

Down went the key.

He tapped out his call sign, one hand pressed tightly to the earphones over his head to receive the go-ahead.

The coded acknowledgment came back in five seconds: "Transmit."

The operator's fingers danced on the keys as he sent the one-word message: "Located!"

Gunfire ripped through the barn as a great light flooded the building through the open door. The radio man was dead before he could sign off. The man at the generator was slammed back off his seat by the impact of the bullets, and the generator was hit and fell on the man's prone body.

Of the two guards at the door, one managed to get off a single shot before his death. The other man was cut down even as he was bringing his pistol up from his side.

The Gestapo unit poured into the cordite-smoking barn, the first soldier ripping the wires from the transmitter. The small slip of paper with its single word was crushed and soaked unrecognizably in the blood of the radio operator.

The last partisan cell in Aosta had been eliminated.

◆   ◆   ◆

The ride to Bancroft's headquarters, in a small villa above Bari, took about half an hour. During that time, Kimball managed to drink a third of the bottle he had brought with him. He could feel it beginning to dull his senses.

McKenzie, behind the wheel of the jeep, caught glimpses of the bottle making its steady journey from lap to lip.

"If you don't mind my saying so, sir," McKenzie said quietly, staring straight ahead at the road, both hands gripping the wheel, "I'd go a bit easy on that stuff. The colonel really has his fuse lit this morning."

"As a matter of fact, Corporal," Kimball said blearily, "I do mind you saying so. And as for the colonel, I hope his goddamned fuse blows him up." He tilted the bottle again.

The remainder of the trip was made in silence, McKenzie stiff-lipped and angry.

The jeep pulled up in front of the villa. Kimball stuffed the bottle into a side pocket of his uniform jacket and untangled himself from the small vehicle. Unsteadily, he made his way to the door and into the cool central hall where several desks were manned by various rates of British Army enlisted personnel.

As Kimball lurched up to the first desk on the right, Sergeant Major Blaisdell looked up, then stood up. As tall as Kimball was at six feet three inches, the massive British senior noncom seemed to tower over him.

"Captain," he announced stonily, "you're drunk!"

Kimball peered red-eyed up at him.

"Sergeant Major, you're out of line," he replied.

Blaisdell signaled to another NCO sitting close by, and then came around the desk and took the Canadian officer by the arm.

"Come along, Captain," he said, almost lifting Kimball from the floor, "let's go get some coffee in you and get you cleaned up a bit." The other NCO took Kimball's other arm.

"Get your goddamned hands off me," Kimball shouted, "or I'll have those stripes nailed to my dart board!"

"Quite right, sir," Blaisdell said evenly, propelling the

Canadian across the room and into a small suite with a bedroom and bath. "And I'd venture to say, if you will permit a small observation, sir, that those pips on your shoulders will probably make an excellent bull's-eye for the board along with our stripes. For that's just where they'll be if I let the colonel see you in this condition."

The two NCOs ushered Kimball into the room, and Blaisdell kicked the door shut. Then he reached for the bottle in the officer's jacket pocket. Kimball drunkenly started a haymaker right that was caught in a bear-trap paw by the huge sergeant major.

Working as if they had been skilled attendants in an alcoholic ward, the two big NCO's deftly stripped Kimball to the nude and then shoved him into the shower. Blaisdell reached in and turned the cold water on full force, then ducked back and planted his huge frame against the shower door. Inside, Kimball cursed and screamed as the water struck him.

"Get along to the mess, Herbie," Blaisdell ordered the other sergeant, "and get a big pot of the black, that's a good fellow. I'll just keep his honor in here until you get back."

He leaned against the door and smiled at the inventiveness of Kimball's language coming through the sounds of the beating shower.

Forty-five minutes later, Kimball was still red-eyed but dressed and clean with a half-gallon of black coffee inside. His head ached furiously, and the aspirin hadn't helped. He swayed only slightly.

He stood in the small room and glared at the two sergeants. "Satisfied?" he snarled.

Silently, Blaisdell surveyed him from head to toe. Then he snapped to attention, foot stamping to the floor and hand swinging palm-up to the side of his head.

"Sir," he cried, "the colonel's compliments, sir, and would you please be so kind as to follow me to his office?"

26

He stamped again, did a perfect about-face and marched from the room, Kimball following. The other sergeant grinned and watched them go.

Colonel George Winsted Bancroft, DSO, VC and chief of British Intelligence (S.O.E.) for Italy, was a product of his family, Oxford, Sandhurst and the War College. In spite of that, he was considered to be one of the finest intelligence officers in the war and one who had the instinctive ability to pick the right man for the right job. In his entire military career no one had seen him smile. Nor had anyone ever publicly heard him express a single word of kindness or sympathy for those who served under his command.

Privately in his own quarters or well away from any other human being, he allowed himself the privilege of abject misery over the loss of any of the men he sent on the many missions the war required.

For six days and nights he had had both his own military people and Italian informers searching Bari and the surrounding towns for Captain Edward Kimball. Now the Canadian officer stood before him, swaying slightly, trying to remain at attention.

Bancroft peered up at him, noting the bloodshot eyes and the slight trembling of hands.

"Good of you to come, Kimball," he said icily. "For God's sake, sit down, man, before you fall down."

Kimball sank into a stiff chair across the desk from the British officer.

"Where the bloody hell have you been?" Bancroft demanded.

"Getting drunk," the Canadian replied.

"Getting drunk, what?" Bancroft roared.

"Getting drunk, *sir,*" Kimball shouted back. Then he clapped his hands to his head and muttered, "Jesus Christ."

"I don't suppose that you'd like to explain the reasons for your behavior, would you?" Bancroft asked.

Kimball glared at the colonel. "You know goddamned well why, Colonel. You send my ass into Bologna with three other good people. Just a little information gathering behind the German lines, you tell me. No sweat, just pop in and pop out. Three days at most. I spent three weeks trying to get my ass out of there, Colonel, and you're looking at the only one who made it. Three good men killed and all because of some goddamned leak in your so-called informant network. And that's the third time you've done that to me.

"Well, for your information, Colonel, as the Americans say in baseball, three times is out. And that's where I am right now. Out. Finito. Finished. Through. That's what I've been getting drunk about, Colonel, sir."

Kimball sat back and glared at his superior officer.

Bancroft listened to the tirade in silence. When Kimball had finished, he leaned back in his chair and studied the haggard Canadian over steepled fingertips. The two men sat in silence for several minutes. Then, as if he had made up his mind, Bancroft nodded to himself and leaned forward.

"I daresay you're right, Captain," he admitted. "It was a bloody cockup, and I'm probably as much to blame as anyone. But I'm not making any excuses. It was a job that had to be done and done in a hurry. We didn't have time to make proper arrangements, but at least you got the job done, and that's what counts."

"Got the job done!" Kimball shouted. "That's what counts? What about three good men dead on the streets? Don't they count? What the hell are you made of, Colonel? Carved out of some floating iceberg off the tip of Iceland? Those men counted, damn it."

"Of course, they did," Bancroft said quietly, "and I had no intention of expunging or minimizing the extent of their loss. But I must remind you that we are in the midst of a shooting war, Captain. Men, poor mud-soaked, cold, wet and frightened sods, are being killed almost every minute.

28

No one likes that, least of all myself. That's why I feel so strongly about this organization and about men like yourself. Yes, three men did die. But, in pulling it off, the four of you managed to save the lives of literally hundreds of those poor sods with the information you got. We could have walked right into a trap.

"And it's for that same reason that you're here now—to try and save even more of them from an even more dangerous trap."

The Canadian stared in amazement at the British intelligence officer.

"I don't believe it," Kimball said slowly. "I don't really believe it. You actually think I'm going to take another of your bloody assignments and get some more people killed. Or maybe you just hope that I'll buy the lot this time. I think you've lost your mind, Colonel."

"I don't particularly give a damn what you believe, Kimball," Bancroft said evenly, "and I know that I can't force you to take a mission, even if I have to court-martial you for refusing. But I bloody well can order you to sit there and keep your mouth shut and listen. And that, Captain, is exactly what I'm doing. Shut up and listen."

Kimball eased his position in the chair and silently sulked, damning his aching head.

"Six days ago," Bancroft said, "and the day we started looking for you, we received a message from one of our agents in northern Italy."

He got up and walked to a map at the side of the room. He pointed to the eastern coast of the boot.

"This is where General Alexander is fighting now, as you well know. We think there's a very good possibility, if this damned weather doesn't hamper him, for our troops to break through the Gothic Line in just a few days. Over here," his finger swung to the left of the boot, "the Americans are making good progress and putting a lot of pressure on Kesselring's right flank. This should be enough for Alexander to break through."

Bancroft turned and looked at the Canadian officer.

"What if the British Army does get through and across the Po?" he asked.

Kimball remained silent.

Again Bancroft pointed to the map.

"Once across the Po," the British officer continued, "the route into Austria and Germany is open to us. If he moves fast, Alexander can ram into the Brenner Pass valley starting at Lake Garda and drive straight for Innsbruck. General Clark and the Americans will swing west and make juncture with the Free French forces now driving into Alsace-Lorraine. We could be in Hitler's backyard by Christmas."

Bancroft came back to his desk and sat down.

"Except for one unknown factor," he said. "For months now our people both in Switzerland and northern Italy have had rumors of massive fortifications the Germans are supposedly building on both sides of the Isarco River valley leading to the Brenner Pass. If those rumors are true, Alexander will be marching into a massive ambush. We have known for some time that the plans for the fortifications and the responsibility for their completion lie with General Wilhelm Meirhausser, who commands Alpengruppe II. Those plans and the timetable for their occupation are in his possession. We must have them, in order to attempt to cut off any further work on the structures and to prevent German forces from occupying them."

Bancroft paused and looked Kimball steadily in the eye.

"Meirhausser's headquarters are in Aosta. More specifically, in the Savoldi Castle, Vulcano Castle, if you will."

Kimball jerked upright at the last comment.

"Our agent has located the plans and so informed us. But before she could give the specific location in the castle, the partisan group that was her transmission facility was overrun by the Gestapo. There has been no further communication.

"Our agent is the Countess Riva di Savoldi, who remains in the castle as its rightful owner and who has gotten the information out of the German command officers situated there."

"You are really a dirty son of a bitch, Colonel," Kimball said slowly, with hate in his voice.

◆　　◆　　◆

Kimball was eight years old and an only child when both his father and mother were killed in an automobile accident on a trip from Edmonton to Winnipeg.

The big prosperous ranch was sold, and four months later young Ed was in Rome with his father's brother and only living relative. Quentin Kimball was a Canadian career diplomat, then with the Canadian consulate in Rome. His uncle and aunt swept him into their family, treated him like their own two boys, one a year older, the other a year younger than Ed.

He grew up with his cousins, all of them attending Italian schools. There was a short stint in Paris for the diplomat, and then back to Rome where he was promoted to senior attaché. The three boys were sent home to Canada for their college years, all attending McGill, Quentin's old school. Then it was back to Italy for both Ed and the older Kimball cousin. Fluent in Italian and French and speaking then a passable German, Ed was introduced by his uncle to a distinguished English gentleman vacationing in Rome. Young Kimball was twenty-two years old and had just come into the considerable fortune that had been building for him from the sale of the vast Canadian ranch, disposed of before the Great Depression struck in the early thirties.

Financially comfortable and no longer a burden upon his aunt and uncle, he was free to find his own niche in life.

The distinguished English gentleman stayed with the Kimballs for three weeks. When he left, he suggested that Ed come to London for a visit.

The year was 1936, the Nazis were rising to power in Germany and the rest of the world was still in the grips of the Depression.

Ed Kimball traveled to London that fall. When he returned to Rome, he held a commission as junior lieutenant in the Canadian Army, detached for unlimited time to British Intelligence.

That winter he met Riva Mangianni on the ski slopes of Saint Moritz. The daughter of a wealthy Italian nobleman and industrialist, she was fascinated by the tall Canadian who spoke Italian as though he had been born in the country. It was a snow-filled whirlwind affair, full of the passion that two young and handsome people could muster and yet without the sense of commitment that either was prepared yet to make. They were ski companions, wealthy play-children and lovers for a month.

Then tenderly, but without bitterness, it was over. She returned to her family in the north of Italy and Ed went back to Rome, both vowing to keep in touch. The following year Riva met and fell madly in love with the dashing Count Milo di Savoldi. They were married shortly thereafter.

To the harassed and tiny staff of British Intelligence, it seemed in 1938 that the only person in the British Isles who failed to recognize the danger of Hitler was Prime Minister Neville Chamberlain. As Hitler gobbled up the Rhineland and Austria, England's envoy of the furled umbrella was making journeys to Munich and coming back filled with tidings of peace.

Chamberlain was not the only one traveling to both Munich and Berlin. Italy's swaggering Il Duce also was crossing the Alps to visit with the Führer and to join Italy's fate with that of the Third Reich.

Ed Kimball spent most of 1938 and the spring and summer of 1939 in the northern Italian Alps. The fiercely independent mountain people had little use for the Blackshirts of Mussolini's Fascist units. Gradually, Kimball built a network of informants who would become the partisan fighters and foes of both Fascists and Nazis during the war years.

He made three visits to the Savoldi castle at Aosta, where he was welcomed as a friend and valued guest by both the count and countess. Riva was obviously deeply in love with her husband and was trying to dissuade him from his naval career so that they could both enjoy the magnificent splendor of their mountain home.

While he was no Fascist and had only disparaging remarks about the party, Savoldi was an ardent Italian nationalist. He was also enough of a realist to see the clouds of war hanging over the Alps.

During Ed's visit to Aosta in the spring of 1939, Savoldi invited him for a day's easy climb in the nearby mountains. The two men worked their way up a gentle face, having fun but not risking their necks. They reached the ridge of the mountain shortly before noon.

From their rucksacks came breads, cheese and wine, and they ate, the magnificent splendor of the valleys and mountains on all sides. When they had finished, they lighted cigarettes.

Savoldi turned to Kimball. "Eduardo, there will be war?"

He made the question sound almost like a statement of fact.

Kimball nodded his head sadly. "Hitler wants war," he replied. "He'll find some excuse to start. And when he does, all of Europe will be involved. Milo, you know I have no great love for your dictator, but I am far less afraid of what he might do than I am of the ex-house painter now in Berlin."

Savoldi digested that comment in silence. "And you English," he asked, "what will you do?"

"I'm Canadian," Ed corrected him with a smile.

Savoldi waved his hand. "That is of no consequence. If England makes war, Canada and all of the Commonwealth are involved. There is talk of troubles along the Polish border. If Hitler crosses into Poland, what will England do?"

"England will honor its pact with Poland," Ed replied. "England will fight. And what of Italy?"

Savoldi shrugged and then crossed himself. "God be with us," he said. "Il Duce will throw us into the war alongside the Germans. Such a terrible thing, friend fighting friend."

Savoldi left the next day to return to his ship.

That night, sitting on the high balcony of Vulcano Castle and watching the twinkling lights of the towns below, Kimball recruited Riva, the Countess di Savoldi, into the British intelligence network.

Blitzkrieg struck Poland that September. Nine months later, Italy entered the war at the side of Germany, and the Axis triumvirate of Germany, Italy and Japan was formed. Great Britain severed diplomatic relations with Italy in June of 1940. By that time, Kimball had established a huge network of future partisan groups throughout northwestern Italy and stretching as far south as Florence. Other S.O.E. agents were putting together similar groups throughout the remainder of Italy.

Milo di Savoldi died less than four months after Italy's entrance into the war against the Allies. From Vulcano Castle, Riva Savoldi was proving a most useful and productive agent.

Kimball saw her once more after war broke out, crossing the Swiss border and slipping from one partisan group to another until he reached Aosta.

In the early winter months of 1941, General Wilhelm

Meirhausser walked through the doors of the Savoldi Castle.

It was Colonel George Bancroft who formulated the scheme for improving information coming out of Vulcano Castle. By this time, Kimball had been transferred briefly to northern France to work with the French Resistance.

Bancroft's plan was simplicity itself. The cold and haughty Italian noblewoman was to thaw gradually in the presence of the handsome and virile German general. In short, Riva Savoldi was to become Meirhausser's mistress, as well as hostess.

For the warm and sensual Italian woman, it was both duty and pleasure.

When the Allies jumped from North Africa to Sicily, Kimball was back operating behind German and Italian lines in Italy. It was on his second mission to the north that he learned that Riva now not only shared her castle but her bed with the German High Command.

It hurt so badly at the time that he couldn't bring himself to report the fact to Bancroft, who was by this time both his boss and controller. He was not sure whether it was his pride or his sense of loyalty that was most bruised. For Riva to become another man's bed partner was one thing. For her to switch loyalties and give herself to a German was even worse. The hurt lingered unchanged over the next three years.

◆   ◆   ◆

Bancroft ignored Kimball's bitter comment.

"Despite your personal views, Captain," the colonel continued, "I would not be putting you into this situation were it not for several factors, prime of which is that you personally are better acquainted with the area than any other man or woman in the organization. You know the partisans, since it was your work that put them together even before this miserable war got started."

"Begging the colonel's pardon," Kimball broke in, "but

there are damned few of those groups still operating up there, fewer yet, so I'm led to believe, because of the shitty weather that has kept us from resupplying them by air."

"That may be true," Bancroft said, "but those still functional can be of assistance to you."

"Colonel, the Gestapo has been building a network of Fascist informants for several years. They have blown or destroyed almost all of the people I knew. You just finished telling me that Riva got out a single-word message and that there's been no further word from her. This would seem to indicate that the Aosta cell has been shot down. These Piedmontese are tough and willing, but they're not stupid. In the face of heavy Gestapo crackdowns and a shortage of resupply by us, if any of them are still alive, they're just keeping their heads down and being good little *paisans*.

"All they want to do is to survive this filthy war, as I do. I have no intention of going up there and trying to persuade them to die for some half-cocked scheme. You can bet that those plans are somewhere in the castle. I've been in that place on a number of visits before the war. There is no way to get in, short of siege artillery and a long fight. It is really a fortress, and as a German Army headquarters, you can also bet there are more graycoats running around there than a dog has fleas."

"I've anticipated most of your arguments," the British intelligence officer said, "and I think I have reasonable solutions for at least two, as well as a third factor which should interest you.

"First, I think we have found a way into Vulcano Castle. On that, more in a moment. Second, we are still in contact with at least one guerrilla partisan unit in the general area which might be persuaded to provide you some assistance. Finally, should you be successful, it would become very obvious that the countess was the source of information, and she would be in jeopardy, much more so than she has already been for the past couple of years. I want you, if at all possible, to extract her, along with the plans."

Bancroft rose and moved towards a rear door of the office. He paused and turned back to Kimball.

"Just let me say, Captain, that I agree with your analysis of both the impregnability of the place and the disarray among the guerrilla units in the area. But it is also apparent, I'm sure even to you, that we neither want another Monte Cassino, in which Vulcano Castle is bombed and shelled to rubble, nor do we have the time or capability for such a project. I think we have found a better way. I might point out to you that despite my somewhat optimistic view of General Alexander's prospects, it's not all that firm. Things are a bit dicey at the moment, since Eisenhower has pulled several divisions out of Italy to support his Anvil operations now pushing up from the Riviera into southeastern France."

He walked to the rear door and opened it. "Please come in, Madame Gaussin."

She was just a couple of inches over five feet tall, thin, wiry and with short-cropped reddish-brown hair. There were faint crow's-feet at the corners of her eyes, and she had the general appearance of one who spent much time outdoors. There was also a wry smile at the corners of her mouth and a sense of self-possession as she entered the room. Kimball rose.

Bancroft escorted her to the desk. "Madame Joelle Gaussin, may I present Captain Edward Kimball?"

She peered up at the tall Canadian, and her face lighted with a bright warm smile. She thrust out her hand. "*Enchanté, Monsieur Capitaine,*" she said. Then in English, "My, but aren't you a big fellow?" Her handshake was firm and dry.

Kimball smiled and pulled another chair around for the Frenchwoman.

Bancroft took his seat behind the desk. "Captain," he

said, "we believe that Madame Gaussin holds the key to our entrance into Vulcano Castle. Both she and her husband, Professor Gaussin, are speleologists of great renown. I assume you are aware of that discipline."

"Cave explorers," Kimball replied with a nod.

"Ah, but not simple explorers," the Frenchwoman cut in. "Ours is not simple curiosity, Captain. We seek some answers to the formations of this earth on which we live and to the extent past developments may safely predict future changes. But also," she paused and laughed merrily, "since we are so often associated with our cave inhabitants, we are just a little . . . what do you say in English . . . a little batty."

Kimball grinned at her.

"For much of the past twenty years," Bancroft continued, "Madame Gaussin and her husband have been working in the many cave systems in the northwestern Italian Alps and foothills and their connecting or correlating systems in eastern France and even in Switzerland. Madame Gaussin and her husband have explored extensively in the Aosta area."

Bancroft walked over to a plank-and-trestle worktable at the side of the room. "Come over here, please."

Kimball and the woman joined him. The British officer unrolled a set of drawings and spread them across the table, weighting the corners with odd bits of paraphernalia.

"These," the colonel said, pointing to the drawings, "are a series of what one might call blueprints of the Savoldi Castle. It is a rare bit of well-preserved architecture dating back to the thirteenth century. A few years before the outbreak of war, the Société Historicale Italia went to some lengths to study many of these old structures still standing. The late Count di Savoldi was an enthusiastic supporter of the enterprise and not only gave them full access to the castle but assisted in much of the exploratory work and some excavation in order to produce these drawings."

Bancroft indicated the top drawing.

"This represents basically the upper or visible portions of the structure, possibly as it existed when first built. Captain Kimball, Madame Gaussin, is familiar with the present layout of these upper works, having been a guest at the castle in the prewar years."

He rolled up the top drawing to reveal a second.

"This represents later additions to the castle as it grew and expanded during the succeeding couple of centuries. These next two drawings show underground works added to the complex. Here is a cistern, used to store water both during dry seasons and possibly during sieges in time of feudal war. Those wars led to the construction of the following."

Again he rolled up the top drawing.

"Against the time that an overwhelming force might storm the castle, the early Savoldis bored a series of tunnels below the cistern and dungeons, leading out of the castle and onto the neighboring slopes. The tunnels, of course, have probably not been used for centuries. During the mapping by the Société, several of them were uncovered, but all with numerous fall-ins and all totally blocked at their exits. Since the builders put many twists and turns into the tunnels to make pursuit difficult, one may only speculate on where they led. Intensive ground search around the castle area failed to reveal a single possible opening. But closer to the castle, they are still in existence, protected from erosion and seepage by their very depth.

"All of which brings us to the Gaussins' most valuable contribution. I would like you to explain that, if you please, Madame Gaussin."

"Before you do, Madame," Kimball said, "I'm beginning to get the picture. But let me tell you, Colonel, that I am no hand at cave exploring and will probably bloody well lose myself and anyone with me if I go in there."

"Not to worry, Captain," Bancroft said. "Madame Gaussin has agreed to accompany you on this mission."

Again Kimball's eyebrows rose. "I would be delighted to have Madame Gaussin's company," he said, "but it would seem to me that this is going to be one hell of a tough project. Might I suggest that possibly Professor Gaussin would be better suited to the job."

Joelle Gaussin shrugged in that fatalistic French way of saying things are terrible. "My husband," she said, "was a professor of science at the University of Grenoble when *les sales Boches* arrived with their French traitors. Jacques was also very politically outspoken. He is now in one of their camps, and I pray to *Le Bon Dieu* that he still lives. Anything, Captain, that will shorten this war and get him back to me is a small thing.

"Besides," she smiled at him, "*I* was the better speleologist of the two of us. Do not fear, I am quite tough, and while I may not be able to reach as high as you, there will be places down there where I can get through but we will have to work most hard to get your great bulk across."

"Enough," Kimball laughed. "I accept your company and your expertise. But I still don't think that this is going to work. Getting to the castle is one thing, Colonel. Getting in is yet another. Getting out is going to be a bitch. We are going to need more manpower."

"We'll get to that in a moment. Please continue, Madame Gaussin."

The Frenchwoman spread out another set of drawings.

"This," she said, pointing to various spots on the drawings, "is a diagram of the cave system that Jacques and I investigated on several occasions. The entrance is here, well covered by brush but easily recognizable because of a pair of tall rock pillars to the left of the opening."

She lifted her hand and indicated the map of northern Italy on the wall above the table.

"The entrance is just about here, some four miles east and north of Savoldi Castle."

She turned back to the cave drawings.

"The system is quite extensive, and we spent a good deal of time trying to determine its full extent. Right here," again her finger picked out a spot on the drawings at the southwestern edge, "we came upon a small and somewhat difficult passage leading in the direction of Aosta. There were a number of rockfalls we managed to climb over or through, but we didn't follow it to the end. However, we did go far enough for me to be convinced, after seeing the drawings Colonel Bancroft has of the castle works, to make me feel certain that we were well into the escape-tunnel system. Quite possibly, had we gone farther, we might have been under the castle itself. This passage inclined upwards to the west for the entire length that we traveled. It could be but a few feet below any one of the underground works of the castle. It is this way that I will take you."

The trio returned to the desk.

"You make it seem like a pleasant little stroll in the dark," Kimball said, "but there's one hell of a lot more to it than that. Assuming that we were to go in, and I'm not saying yet, Colonel, that that's a foregone conclusion. Just how do you expect us to get there?"

"To begin," Bancroft said, "there will be a third member of your party going in. You'll meet him shortly, and before you do, there are some facts about him that you will have to know. But to answer your question, we plan on flying you in for a C-47 drop."

"That's great," Kimball said bitterly, "just great. The weather up there this time of year is so shitty—my pardon, Madame . . ."

"*C'est rien,*" she smiled at him. "Wait until you hear me curse in French."

"The weather is so bad," Ed continued, "that we can't

41

even supply our partisan groups, yet you intend to drop us in by 'chute."

Kimball turned to the woman. "I hope your life insurance is paid up, Madame Gaussin," he said.

Again a Gallic shrug. "My insurance, my *raison d'être*, if you will," she replied, "sits in a German concentration camp. If he should not survive, I have no great concern about continuing."

"Fine," Kimball said sadly, "you are resigned. I'm not so sure about my own postwar plans, but I'd sure like to make some. But just for the sake of discussion, Colonel, let's assume that we do make the drop, we do get in and get the plans. How in God's world do we get out? There isn't twenty feet of flat ground up there for an air pickup, and the weather is almost certain to be so bad that even if there were a landing spot, we'd never know when to make contact."

"Understood," Bancroft said. "You also know, Captain, that Aosta is less than thirty-five miles south of the Swiss frontier. I would expect you to plan on getting out on foot and across that border. Once out of the castle, you will be traveling light, only what you need for the short trip and little or no equipment. And as I said earlier, I sincerely hope —no, I expect—that you will have the support of at least one active partisan group in that area. But again, let's hold that for a minute. Anything other than that?"

"Oh, not really," Kimball replied with a shrug. "All we have to do is to make our way on foot, uphill, into the snowbelt, across the mountains and down into Switzerland with half of the German Army looking for us or chasing us uphill into the arms of the Nazi ski patrols along the frontier. No, sir, I guess that really covers all the problems."

Bancroft glared stonily at Kimball for a full ten seconds. "All through, Captain? Your sarcasm is being wasted. I've seen you work out escape routes much more difficult than this, so let's get down to some serious planning."

Kimball was torn between getting up and telling Bancroft to shove his mission and the image of Riva's face in his mind. He half-rose from his chair and then settled back with a resigned sigh.

"All right, Colonel, let's do some planning. Can we talk about this alleged partisan unit that's going to come rushing out waving the Union Jack in welcome when we arrive?"

Again Bancroft ignored the danger signals. "In just a few minutes you will be meeting the third member of your team. It is important that you both know beforehand some background information on this young man.

"His name is Sergeant Vincent Marco, and he's an American on loan to us for this particular mission. He has been picked, as a matter of fact, Captain, on a small bit of information you obtained several years ago. He comes to us from the American combat engineers, and he is a demolitions expert, both in the service and in civilian life. He's young and quite a hard-bitten fellow, from what they tell me of his recent training at our commando camp. I would think he will be of inestimable value in your passage through both the caves and tunnels, inasmuch as the only possible means of getting through severe rockfalls and breaking into the tunnel system may be through the use of small but well-placed explosive charges.

"But Sergeant Marco is playing a double role for us, one that he is presently unaware of but one which made his selection from the thousands of persons available most urgent. I am going to give you his background, and I will let you, Captain, give him certain facts when you deem it the proper moment."

For the next several minutes, Bancroft reviewed Marco's personal history. When he had finished, Kimball sat in silence for a moment.

"I've got to say this about you, Colonel," he finally spoke up, "you may be the world's coldest bastard, but you

43

certainly do your homework. This just might be the kind of thing Cosimo would buy, put his neck and those of his partisan group on the line for. You're sure the kid doesn't know any of this?"

"Positive," Bancroft replied. "He's a pretty tough and cynical young New Yorker. He thinks he's been recruited simply because he speaks Italian and there's some dirty demolition job to be done on a bridge, or something of that order, behind enemy lines. Now, let's meet this young man, and then I'm going to leave the three of you alone. Get on with your planning, and please have a list of supplies you think you'll need ready for me by this time tomorrow. With any kind of decent 'met' report, you'll go out two nights from now."

He picked up his desk phone and spoke briefly to the sergeant major in the outer office. Moments later, there was a knock at the door.

On Bancroft's command it opened, and Sergeant Vincent Marco walked into the room, stopped five paces from the desk and threw a sloppy salute in Bancroft's general direction.

"Sergeant Vincent Marco, reporting as ordered, sir."

Bancroft came around the desk, returning the salute and holding out his hand. Kimball also rose.

"Thank you for coming, Sergeant. Please meet Madame Joelle Gaussin and Captain Edward Kimball. Captain Kimball is Canadian, you know."

Instinctively, as they grasped hands, Marco and Kimball started sizing each other up. Kimball liked what he saw.

Marco was short but built like a wrestler. His dark curly hair framed an olive-complexioned face with heavy dark eyebrows, deep brown eyes, a Romanesque nose that was slightly askew from a teenaged street brawl. He was broad in shoulder, and even under the winter uniform jacket heavy muscles bulged in both upper and lower arms. His grip was crushing.

44

He was mumblingly polite to Joelle. Bancroft had pulled another chair up beside those of Kimball and the Frenchwoman. He indicated that Marco should take it. The young American seated himself and tried to look bored.

"You three," Bancroft said, "are now a team. Captain Kimball will head it, Sergeant, with Madame Gaussin coming along for technical help that you will be told about in moments. But should anything happen to the captain, I expect you to know as much about the plans as possible and to make every effort to carry out the mission yourself. Now I'll leave you three to get on with your planning."

"Before you go, Colonel," Kimball said, "have you got a name for this mission for requisition purposes?"

"As a matter of fact, I have. It would seem most appropriate to call this the Proserpine Mission."

Marco looked blank.

"Proserpine, Sergeant," Bancroft said, "was a beauteous lady out of early Greek mythology. One of the gods of the underworld fell in love with her and confined her in his castle in hell. She was later rescued by Mercury—which now becomes Captain Kimball's code name and which you would assume should he fall."

Kimball grinned wryly. "In order to rescue her, Sergeant, Mercury had to go to hell. And to do that, I suppose he had to be dead. Most appropriate, Colonel. We'll send you a postcard from hell."

Bancroft glared but did not reply. He walked out of the office.

Kimball heaved a small sigh, unbuttoned his tunic and fished out cigarettes. Both Joelle and Marco accepted one, and they all lighted up and waited for Kimball to begin.

For the next half hour, Kimball reviewed for Marco all that Bancroft had said, including Joelle taking the American GI through the blueprint and cave drawings.

"In order to make this thing work," Kimball concluded, "we're going to have to have some local assistance. There's one partisan group in the area which might help us." He glanced at his watch. His head was still pounding slightly. "Why don't we adjourn this session to the taverna across the road?" he suggested. "I could do with a drink and some more coffee."

Joelle Gaussin sensed that there Kimball would bring Marco completely into the picture. It was something that should be kept à deux.

"With your permission, Captain, I should love to join you, but there are some matters and a couple more drawings back at my quarters that I should get. Why don't I pick them up and meet you both back here in, say, an hour?"

Kimball smiled gratefully at the sensitive Frenchwoman. "A fine idea. We'll meet in an hour. But before we break up right now, let's get a little more informal. The three of us are going to be up to our necks in trouble for several days, starting very shortly. I will head up the team, but during that time, rank doesn't mean a damn thing. So starting right now—with the exception, of course, in the presence of the distinguished colonel—my name is Ed."

"And I am Joelle, Ed," she smiled and said with her slight accent.

"Is it Vincent?" Ed asked Marco.

The Italian-American soldier had been listening and watching Kimball closely during the briefing. He had almost made up his mind that he could trust the guy. Now he looked at Kimball for a moment as if making a decision.

"My friends back home," he said, "call me Vinnie."

A few minutes later, Ed and Vinnie were seated at a rear table in the little taverna across from S.O.E. headquarters, a small cognac before Kimball and a large tumbler of red wine for the American.

"Let me tell you about the man we hope to enlist when we get up there," Kimball said after taking a small sip of the cognac. "His code name is Cosimo, and I met him several

46

years ago, just before the war. If it's any measure of confidence, Vinnie, I know northern Italy very well." Without changing pace, Kimball had switched to fluent Italian.

Marco raised an eyebrow and nodded his head, while shaking his loose right hand in front of him in a typical Italian gesture of approval. "You sound almost like you were born here," he said.

"I grew up in Italy," Ed explained, "and I've spent a good many years of my life here. It was my job, both before the war and after it started, to develop the partisan groups in northern Italy. Cosimo was one of the first I recruited. He's tough and mean and built like a barrel, a lot like you, Vinnie, but taller. During the time I spent with him, and that was on several occasions, he mentioned that he had once lived in America as an immigrant. In this business, anything you can pick up to give you a background check on the loyalty and honesty of a person is useful. In any case, we asked our American OSS friends to have a look at Cosimo's American period. It turned out most interesting.

"Cosimo came to New York in the late twenties and settled into the Italian community there. He met a girl and married her. Being strong and tough, he found work on the waterfront as a stevedore. The money wasn't great in those days, but a dollar went farther. They managed. Late one afternoon, after his gang had completed loading a freighter, they all adjourned for a couple of quick drinks at the nearby waterfront bar before heading home. One of the dockwallopers, a huge Irishman with a reputation as a heavy drinker, had quit the job early and had been in the bar for more than an hour when the rest of the gang arrived. By that time, he had enough in him to be half drunk.

"For some reason, the Irishman started in on Cosimo, first just needling him as a wop who couldn't speak English properly. And that was true. Cosimo was learning, but he still spoke with a heavy Italian accent and many English words went over his head. But Cosimo took this with good nature. It wasn't until the Irishman started making nasty remarks about Cosimo's family that the trouble began. Whatever it was, the two started fighting. The Irishman was big, but Cosimo was broader and stronger. When the Irishman grabbed Cosimo in a bear hug and tried to gouge out an eye, Cosimo kneed him in the balls. When the Irishman howled and doubled over, Cosimo hit him as hard as he could alongside the head. The Irishman was dead before he hit the floor, his neck snapped. Cosimo was panic-stricken. An Italian immigrant, not even an American citizen and not speaking the language, all he could see was prison.

"He took all of the money out of his pocket except for a couple of dollars and gave it to one of his gang to deliver to his wife. He told the man to tell his wife he would send for her when he could. Then he took off. Somehow, he found an Italian freighter leaving the next day. He talked the mate into taking him aboard as a deckhand, just for passage back to Italy. So Cosimo came back to Italy, slipping off the ship in Naples and making his way back to the north. But by this time the Depression was on and everyone was starving, particularly in Italy. Cosimo never did get the money to send for his wife and little boy. They went to live with relatives, and his wife died four years later."

Kimball paused, then knocked back the rest of the cognac and called for another. Marco just sat there in silence, the first glimmerings of what Kimball was saying beginning to take form in his mind.

Ed waited until the waiter had brought the new drink and then took half of it with a gulp. He set the glass down and looked back at Vinnie.

"Vinnie, Cosimo's real name is DeMarco, and you were just six years old when he took off for Italy. Your mother dropped the first syllable of the name. Cosimo is your father, kid."

Marco looked as though he had been struck by a club. He was stunned and dazed, and his eyes appeared not to be able to focus on Kimball.

Then the film fell from his eyes, and deep hatred glowed.

"That dirty asshole," he said with cold, deadly fury. "He let my ma die, left me to starve. And never, never one goddamned word from him all these years. She'd never tell me anything about him, except that she always believed he'd send for us. Nothing, I tell you, nothing! She died still calling for him, begging him to come for us, pleading for him to save her. Nothing."

Marco raged for a half hour, and Kimball listened in silence. When the first shock had passed, only hatred remained.

"And you expect *me* to go up there and *ask* that bastard to help us? You're outta your mind, Kimball. I'll kill the son of a bitch if I get within three feet of him, that's what I'll do. I'll kill him."

"I'm sorry, Vinnie," Kimball said. "This wasn't my idea. But I couldn't let you go in there without knowing the truth."

"I'll bet my ass this is something that iceberg prick Bancroft thought up," Marco muttered angrily. "I tell you, I'll kill him if you get me close enough."

Kimball shrugged. "So maybe you will," he said, "and maybe you won't. Don't worry, I'll get you close enough. But I can tell you this, Vincente DeMarco, if you do, you blow our only chance of pulling this thing off, and if we blow it, there are going to be one hell of a lot of GIs dead because of it."

Marco lapsed into a black silence.

"I want to say one last thing," Ed said to the morose young American, "and then we'll drop the subject. Regardless of whether we get help or not, I intend to make the attempt, even if there only are the three of us. I don't think

49

we can do it, but I swear, Vinnie, that we're going to try. So straighten your head around and help."

Throughout the remainder of the day and well into the night, the trio worked out the list of supplies they would need for the task. About one in the morning, Kimball called a halt and inspected the growing inventory.

"Look at this," he exclaimed, holding the sheet for the other two to see. "If we took this much in, it would take an army to transport it. So now we start trimming."

When they completed their planning, they were down to four fifty-pound drop packages. Two of them would contain mostly closely packed half-pound blocks of nitrostarch explosive. The detonators went into the third pack, along with two nylon climbing ropes, German uniforms and a four-day supply of K-rations in their waxed Crackerjack boxes. Also included were four heavy four-foot-long crowbars and a pair of mountain axes. Gas masks and tear-gas containers were also packed.

Extra thirty-round ammunition clips for the three M-3 "grease gun" submachine guns they would carry on the jump were wedged in with the nitrostarch. The submachine guns were the paratroop-adapted version with a folding-frame shoulder stock.

"What do we wear?" Marco asked.

"American combat fatigues and jump boots, down jackets and dark wool caps. It's going to be damned cold up there in the hills, even this time of year. And if we get picked up, it doesn't matter what we're wearing anyway. We're going to be shot."

The Proserpine team caught five hours of sleep and then spent most of the day packing the padded drop bags with the supplies that Bancroft kept streaming in through the morning hours.

Rain again fell throughout the day, and darkness came early in the cold October night. By that time, they were ready.

The hardest task had been to find a set of American fatigues and jump boots small enough to fit the diminutive Joelle. Even the smallest set bagged around her, and she grimaced at her image in the lav mirror as she dressed for the mission.

All lights were out at the rear of the villa when the truck backed to the door to load the drop packs and the Proserpine team. They loaded quickly and were bounced and jostled for more than two hours from Bari to a high-security Fifteenth Air Force Special Groups base outside of Brindisi.

The C-47 was waiting on the line when the truck backed to the rear door. From some unknown source, Bancroft had managed to find a dozen rolls of a new fluorescent tape, just being produced by an American company. Now, each of the four drop packs was striped on all sides with the tape. The drop bags were stowed at the rear of the aircraft opposite the door, and the trio boarded. Their 'chutes were already aboard. Moments later the door was closed, and the twin-engined C-47 lumbered down the darkened runway and lifted slowly and awkwardly into the cloud cover. Weather forecasts gave them slightly better than a fifty-fifty chance of finding an opening in the cloud cover over their drop zone, north and east of Aosta.

Throughout the bumpy flight northward, Kimball drilled Joelle in the use of the parachute packs.

"There's nothing to it, Joelle," he explained. "All you have to do is jump the moment I yell. There's a static line on the back of your pack that hooks onto that cable running the length of the cabin. When you hit the end of the line, it will pull the pack cover off and pull out the top of the 'chute. Three turns of string will break, and the pack cover is left dangling behind the plane, and your 'chute will be open."

He explained how to haul on the suspension lines from the canopy in order to steer the 'chute. "Keep your legs loose. The instant you hit the ground, let yourself fall and roll. The 'chute will hit the ground and collapse. Then you unsnap the D-rings and get out of the harness."

She smiled up at him. "It will be a new experience for me, *mon ami.*"

Kimball checked Marco out on 'chute procedure. The American had already made a half-dozen jumps in commando training. "What about chest pack reserves?" he asked.

Kimball looked up the cabin to where Joelle sat. "No point in them," he said softly. "We're going to drop at eight hundred feet. If this thing doesn't work, there isn't time to pull a reserve."

"Jesus Christ," Marco muttered.

Satisfied that he had given them as much information as possible on their landing zone and parachute use, Kimball again reviewed all of the plans for the mission, against the possibility of his own death or capture.

Joelle listened intently, but Marco seemed aloof and distracted. Faced with the immediate problems of getting out of the plane and safely on the ground with their equipment, he was still caught up in his shadow-memory hatred of the man who was his father.

After Kimball started the review for the third time, Marco blew up. "Shit, Captain, I'm no moron. How many goddamned times do you have to say something to think that I pick up on it?"

"Just as goddamned many times as I think it necessary until I get some idea that your mind isn't a million miles away, Vinnie. What the hell's the matter with you, *paisane?* You getting cold feet?"

"Fuck you, Captain," Marco growled at him. "I'll go anywhere you can go and probably one hell of a lot of places that would wipe your ass out."

Kimball grinned. "That's better. You're back. Now let's cut out this 'captain' crap and get back to being a team."

Marco lapsed into silence but listened carefully.

It was a rough spine-wrenching five-hour flight to the drop zone. Try as they did, there was no way even to catnap on the trip up. They were to be over the drop zone at approximately three-thirty in the morning. Kimball wanted the darkness hours to hide their parachutes and drop packs before setting out in search of Cosimo.

The foothills of the Pennine Alps behind Aosta afforded very few clear drop zones, even in good weather and reasonable visibility.

Tonight it was raining, and the valleys were patched with fog. The C-47 pilot had been over the area several times, making supply drops for partisan groups, and he assured them he knew the terrain well. What he didn't tell them was that often the supply drops were made miles from where the waiting partisan groups had been assembled. They were often lost forever. At least people who dropped should be able to walk to the right area, even if the drop was a bit off. If, of course, they survived the landing and weren't spotted by German troops.

A half hour before jump time, the pilot and crew chief came back into the main cabin. They had started their slow descent into the Valle D'Aosta. And this meant flying through rain and fog below the tops of some of the mountains.

"It may look a little hairy," the boyish Air Force officer in his leather flight jacket said, "but not to worry. We've done this dozens of times."

Privately, Kimball translated that to mean he had been into the area at least twice.

Now conversation was almost impossible. The crew chief had opened the rear door of the cabin and locked it back against the hull. The roar of the wind and the big droning engines effectively drowned out all but shouting.

Ed moved to the open door and lay down on the floor, his head wrenched by the slipstream and soaked by the driving rain. He could see nothing but clouds. Then there was a break, and he thought he saw the dim reflection of water below. It could be the Dora Baltea River that flowed past Aosta.

He pulled back into the plane and glanced at his watch. At that moment, a yellow light shone above the open door. He waved to his two companions, and they both rose, buckle of the static line in the left hand, the right against the bucking cabin wall to keep their balance.

"Hook up," Ed yelled.

He snapped his own static line to the overhead cable, as did Joelle and Marco.

The crew chief put his mouth against Kimball's ear. "We'll be making two passes over the DZ," he shouted. "The bundles go out on the first pass, you guys on the second."

Ed nodded.

The light above the door changed from yellow to red. Each of them stood ready.

One minute later the light flashed green. The crew chief heaved out the first drop bag, and with a mighty kick Kimball shoved the next one after it. Marco's followed immediately, and by that time the crew chief had the fourth bundle at the door. It went out. The green light winked off and turned to yellow.

Kimball signaled to his companions, and they moved to the door, Joelle standing blinking into the roaring wind. She would go first, followed by Marco, and Ed would bring up the rear. The C-47 was in a tight bank, and they clutched for support. Then it leveled off, and the light again was red.

"Stand by," Ed shouted.

Joelle placed her hands on the edges of the door, all fingers outside as Kimball had instructed her, pressing against the cold outer-hull metal of the aircraft.

Green light.

"Go," Kimball yelled, "go."

One after the other, Joelle and Marco plunged out of the door. Kimball was close enough behind Marco to touch his pack in midair as he followed.

Even with the C-47 throttled down for the few seconds of the jump, the slipstream tore at their faces and bodies. They had stowed their wool caps in jacket pockets to keep them from being blown away, and their submachine guns were strapped against their chests.

Five seconds.

Kimball felt the welcoming jerk of the parachute harness as the canopy blossomed out ahead of him. He swung under it and reached up to check the swings. For the first time, he looked down. In the dark, he thought he could make out the outlines of a small clearing, surrounded by trees on all sides. Even with the C-47 now long gone, the wind was blowing hard.

At eight hundred feet on a static line jump, there is just time enough between the opening of the 'chute and meeting the ground for the canopy to check the fall and allow two huge pendulum swings under the canopy. Then the jumper is down.

They struck on the side of a hill in a high wind. Ed had checked his swing as he hit and tumbled. He rolled over and hauled in on the 'chute lines, collapsing the twenty-eight-foot nylon canopy.

A few feet distant, Joelle lay on her back, motionless; her 'chute, luckily, collapsed as its edge struck the ground.

There was no sign of Marco.

Kimball worked frantically at his harness fastenings, then ran to the Frenchwoman's side. He gave a quick tug at the lower suspension lines to take the last pocket out of the blowing canopy and then reached for the harness snaps on her small figure.

Her eyes opened and she blinked. "Whooo," she gasped, "*c'est formidable.*"

Ed gave a sigh of relief as he unsnapped the last harness catch.

"You OK, Joelle?" he asked anxiously.

She sat up and tentatively tried her arms and legs, then ruefully rubbed a bruise at the back of her head. "I think so. I just had the breath knocked out of me. You didn't say it would be so strong," she said accusingly and then smiled. "But I did it, *non?*"

Ed grinned at her and helped her to her feet.

"You certainly did, *chéri*. Come on, let's see if we can find Vinnie. I hope he's not caught in some treetop."

They picked their way down the darkened slope in the direction of the wind. It was Joelle who spotted the white of the parachute.

"There," she exclaimed.

They found the American sergeant at the base of a tree, unconscious. The wind had slammed him into the trunk, and blood was oozing from a scalp wound.

Kimball felt for a pulse. "He's alive," he told Joelle, "just knocked out."

Kimball suddenly stopped and stood, straining into the whistling wind. Faintly and at a distance, it carried the high whine of a siren.

"Let's move fast," he called to Joelle. "I think someone may have spotted us."

He reached down and eased the harness from Marco's still body and left him there.

"He'll be all right until we come back. Come on, Joelle, we've got to find those bundles and get them out of sight."

It took them a half hour to find all four bundles, and it was Bancroft's idea that saved the mission. Using his penlight, Ed found each of the drop bags in the dark as the thin beam of light flickered across a strand of orange fluorescent tape. But it took them more time than that to heave each one of them down the slope and into a ravine where Kimball covered them with fallen brush and limbs. Twice he thought

56

he saw the distant glow of lights against the low-hanging clouds.

Tiredly, the man and woman made their way back to where Marco still lay unconscious.

"His pulse is stronger and he's breathing better," Ed said as he wrapped a surgical field dressing around the scalp wound at the back of Marco's head. "But we've got to get him out of here."

He looked around. Now the light was glowing just over the ridge below them, the tip of a searchlight beam probing the area. He thought the wind carried the faint sound of voices.

Racing back to their 'chutes, he bundled all three and jammed them under nearby brush, several hundred yards from where the drop bags lay hidden.

"Help me," he said as he pulled Marco to a sitting position. He knelt down and, with her assistance, got the American across his shoulders and strained to his feet.

"Come on," he ordered and moved away from the lights angling downward into the trees. Joelle stumbled quickly after him, carrying Marco's submachine gun along with her own.

The sky was beginning to lighten, and Kimball knew that they had but little time to find a hiding place from the patrols before dawn.

Rain had stopped falling while they were concealing the bags, and the clouds had broken long enough for him to pick out two prominent peaks and take a cross-bearing on them with his pocket compass. But he was puzzled by the first sound of the sirens. If they were coming from Aosta, it was the wrong direction.

They stumbled and pushed their way deeper into the forest along the lower slopes of the mountains. Now they no longer heard the sound of voices or saw lights. But the sky was losing its dense blackness.

For more than a mile, he led the way, finally tripping

and barely catching himself before falling with the heavy Marco. He slid to the ground, exhausted, Marco lying beside him. Joelle slumped beside him.

"Gotta rest," he panted. "My God, but he's a heavy bastard."

When his breath returned, he signaled Joelle to remain with Marco and then probed through the nearby trees. He almost fell off the edge of a cliff, grabbing a tree limb at the last second. Far below him, in the growing light, was the narrow band of the Dora Baltea River—and they were on the wrong side of Aosta. Mentally, he cursed the hotshot pilot who had flown "dozens" of missions into these mountains. But at least he had some idea of where they were. Kneeling at the base of a tree and shielding the tiny beam with his body, he examined a map from his jacket pocket. Then he rose and went back to the others. Marco was moving and moaning slightly.

Again he managed to get the American on his back and, with Joelle trotting behind, threaded his way through the trees, paralleling the edge of the cliff but several hundred yards above it. In another ten minutes he found what he had been seeking.

A rockfall had smashed through the trees, snapping trunks and limbs into a jumble and then piling huge broken boulders over the fallen trees. He put Marco down and searched along the edge of a fall. Between two broken trunks was an aperture. He crawled in and felt around. It was big enough for the three of them.

With Joelle's aid, he managed to drag Marco into the opening. He shoved Joelle inside and then gathered as many broken branches as possible. He stacked them over the opening and left a couple outside. Squeezing through the now-narrowed hole, he squirmed around and reached out for the last of the limbs. Carefully, he maneuvered it over the remaining small opening. Only a filtering of light came through the covering.

Marco's eyes flickered open, and he moaned softly.

◆　◆　◆

The two-man German motor patrol had been cruising slowly through the rain on the rutted dirt road along the river's edge. The roar of the Volkswagen engine and the drumming of the rain made conversation almost impossible.

The trooper sitting beside the driver in the enclosed vehicle turned to his companion.

"Hans, rain or no rain, I've got to take a leak. Stop this thing, will you?"

The driver grinned and kept his eyes on the narrow muddy trail. "You're going to get soaked if you get out in that," he shouted, "so just piss in your pants. No one will know the difference."

High above the river road, the throttled-down C-47 was making its first pass over the area, but the sound of the plane was lost over the roar of the VW engine and the beat of the rain.

"Come on, Hans," the other soldier said. "That's not even funny. Stop this damned thing and let me out. Look, the rain is letting up." The driver slowed the vehicle and then brought it to a stop. The rain stopped at the same moment.

The trooper climbed hurriedly from the jeep and moved to a tree at the side of the road, frantically fumbling with the buttons on his fly. With a sigh, he urinated happily against the tree. The driver had shut off the engine and it was quiet in the hills, except for the burbling of the river near at hand and the drip of raindrops falling from the trees. The rains had stopped, and the cloud cover broke for at least a few minutes. The trooper was just buttoning up to get back into the vehicle when the C-47 came around on its second pass above the valley. Startled, the soldier peered up the mountains.

"Hans," he yelled, "listen."

The sound of the plane's engines changed to a lower pitch, and for a split second the Wehrmacht sentry thought he caught a brief glimpse of its silvery form. Then the engines went back to a high-pitched roar and began fading in the distance. It was then that the soldier spotted the faint outlines of parachute canopies just above the trees, high above him.

He raced for the jeep. "Get down to the river sentry box, Hans," he shouted. "I think I just saw some parachutes coming down up there. You heard the plane, didn't you?"

The driver nodded and gunned the jeep down the muddy road with disregard for holes or rocks. Of all the nights to have a damned vehicle with a dead radio. It took them almost twenty minutes to get to the sentry box that stood at the river road junction beside the bridge that crossed the Dora Baltea. There was a direct phone line to the castle. Two minutes later, the sirens jerked both General Meirhausser and Major Koppfman out of their sleep. Still in robes, both men reached the duty desk at the same instant.

"What's happening?" the general called out.

"Parachutes, Herr General. One of our patrols spotted them on the west slope just a few minutes ago. They also heard the plane."

"I told you," Koppfman snarled as he hurried to his office. "This killing thing has stirred the hornet's nest. Now we've got agents or supplies dropping in for the partisans."

He began calling his Gestapo staff and getting the word out to all informants.

The Wehrmacht colonel commanding the several hundred headquarters troops came hurrying in, hastily buttoning his tunic. Hard on his heels was the Waffen SS major in charge of a slightly smaller contingent of the Death's Head unit.

The pair joined Meirhausser at the large-scale map of the area on the wall, along with the senior noncom who had taken the call from the sentry box.

The *feldwebel* pointed to the map. "I talked with the man who made the sighting, Herr General. He estimates that it took them about twenty minutes to reach the phone. In the dark and rain, they couldn't have been driving over thirty kilometers an hour. That would have put them about here when Gerhardt saw the plane and the parachutes. He said they appeared to be several thousand feet above him, up that west slope."

Meirhausser studied the map for a minute. "All right," he said to the two officers at his side, "let's get the men out. I want a tight perimeter on that entire area from above where the soldier thinks he saw them down to the river. They can't get across the river without using the bridge this time of year. Use every available man."

"It's going to be footwork, General," the Wehrmacht colonel said, looking at the map. "There aren't more than a couple of trails up in that area, and it's heavily wooded."

"I know that, you fool," Meirhausser snarled. "Get those men out there on their hands and knees if they have to, but I want to know if anyone dropped in, and, if so, I want them in my hands. Understood?"

The colonel snapped to attention.

"*Zu befehl,* Herr General," he shouted and then ran from the hall.

The Waffen commander had heard enough and raced after his Wehrmacht counterpart.

Meirhausser went back to his room to dress. By this time, the entire castle complement was on the move as the search was organized.

Ever since sending her final message and learning that her communications group had been slain by the Gestapo, Riva had been tormented by the question of whether the message had ever been received, even transmitted. But the execution of the partisan group had also ended her usefulness, and she withdrew not only from Meirhausser's bed but to within herself.

The sirens awakened her. She peered from her darkened room and saw men hurrying in the main courtyard. The sounds of truck and jeep engines seeped through the closed windows. The rain had stopped for a moment.

She opened her door and stepped into the corridor. From the main hall, she heard Meirhausser shouting but couldn't make out his words. Silently, she slipped back into her room and began dressing. She heard the hurried slip-slap of Meirhausser's slippers as he ran back to his room to get into uniform.

Riva waited a full hour and then walked out and downstairs. It was a bedlam of men listening to field phones, getting radio messages, shouting orders and hurrying by. No one paid attention to her. She walked to the rear of the big hall. The door to Koppfman's office was ajar, and she could hear both the Gestapo man and Meirhausser talking. She inched closer, glancing about, but still found no one paying heed to her.

"There's no question about it, General," Koppfman said. "It was enemy agents. They found three parachutes and harnesses up there. If it had been supplies, they would have either dropped them without parachutes or the parachutes would still be attached to a supply bundle. These are people, at least three, though there may be more parachutes we haven't found."

"We've got every man possible up there," Meirhausser's voice boomed. "I don't think they can get out of the area before we find them. It's getting light now, and they should be easier to spot if they try to move about."

Riva shuddered with pleasure at the information. The message had gotten out. Someone was trying to reach her. She continued to listen.

"I've got all of my men out as well," Koppfman said. "We're getting the word to every informant in the area about the drop, and I've told my people to say that there will be a ten thousand-lire reward for anyone giving us information.

"I've also got the printing shop running off circulars that should be ready in about an hour. We'll blanket the area with them by noon. They tell of the reward and say that we will shoot any man, woman or child who gives shelter to any of these spies. Oh, we'll find them, Herr General, never fear. We'll find them."

"I'm sure we will, Major," Meirhausser said, "and then we'll shoot them."

"We may shoot them finally, Herr General," Koppfman corrected him, "but not before we in the Gestapo have had a chance to question them. I want to know what they're doing here, and if I have to pull their fingers off one at a time, I will find out."

There was a long silence.

"May I remind the general," Koppfman continued, "that our beloved Führer himself has given orders that all enemy agents captured are to be turned over to the Gestapo for questioning in any fashion that the Gestapo feels will most encourage talking?"

"I know the directive, Koppfman," Meirhausser said angrily, "but that doesn't mean that I have to like it."

"Like it or not . . ." Koppfman said.

Riva silently walked away from the door and back up to her room. She threw back the drapes and stared out at the gray clouds hanging below the mountain peaks. A gray dawn was giving way to the gray of another wet day. The rain again was falling.

Kimball clapped a hand over Marco's mouth and put his fingers to his own lips. The American's eyes looked up at him for a moment, and then he nodded slightly. Kimball removed his hand.

"Where are we?"

Quickly, in whispers, Kimball brought him up-to-date.

Now it was full gray light, and the rain was falling against the piled-up limbs at the entrance to their den. A small rivulet trickled in and pooled on the dirt floor.

They stayed in the hole throughout the day. They could hear the German foot patrols crashing through the underbrush of nearby trees and the occasional muttered oath as a wet helmeted soldier tripped. But none came within fifty yards of the den. By midafternoon, it had been nearly three hours since they had heard a sound.

The bleeding cut on Marco's scalp had closed, and Joelle replaced the big field dressing with a small piece of tape and gauze. Marco winced as she tried to clean the wound.

"It is really quite small, Vincent," she reassured him. "With this little bandage, you may now put on your wool cap."

At four o'clock, Kimball decided to take a chance on fixing their present location. Inch by inch, he carefully moved the limbs from the front of the den until he had a hole big enough to ease his head and shoulders through. He crawled on his belly into the opening and lay for a second with his head outside, listening. There was only the sound of the rain.

He eased out of the den and looked around. If he had been right during the night, the river lay to his left and the cliff would not be more than a couple of hundred yards distant. He crept away from the rock into the blending shadows of the trees and brush, and squirmed his way forward. He reached the cliff's edge in ten minutes.

One look was all he needed. Below him was the river, and to the right, about two miles downstream, was the bridge. He knew exactly where they were. Kimball squirmed his way back to the den.

"You feel up to moving?" he asked the Italian-American soldier.

"You lead, I follow."

64

At dusk, the trio cautiously worked its way through the trees and down the slope, heading for the floor of the valley. If there was still a search on for them in the immediate area, it was not evident.

It was close to ten at night when Kimball called a halt. The three crouched in the dark.

"In just a short while," Ed said, "we come to a farmhouse. It's owned by a chap named Lucca—used to be one of a partisan group I formed. But the Gestapo got onto them. Caught them all on a mission one night, the night Lucca stayed home because his wife was having a baby. I guess no one squealed on Lucca, but they were all executed. As far as I know, he's still here. I think I can trust him long enough to put us up for a night, but Vinnie, you and I sleep in shifts, keeping an eye on him just in case. OK?"

Marco and Joelle nodded.

Kimball knocked gently at the door of the ancient small farmhouse, then he moved back into the dark beside the door. There was no answer. He moved around to the side where he knew Lucca and his wife slept. Again he knocked, this time on the closed shutters. In a moment a man's voice called out.

"Lucca, come to the door. It's Eduardo."

In seconds the front door swung open. Not a light shone in the house. The mustachioed farmer peered into the darkness.

"Eduardo?" he called softly.

"Here," Kimball said, and the farmer jumped.

"Holy Mother of God," he exclaimed. "It is you. I had no idea it would be you when the word got out today that there were secret agents around. Eduardo, this is very dangerous. They look everywhere for you."

"May we come in, Lucca? There are three of us. Just until dawn. We're tired and hungry and need to rest. I promise you we'll be gone in the morning."

The farmer hesitated for a moment and then stepped back.

"Just until morning, Eduardo. And no lights. People might see them and wonder why I was up at such an hour."

"That's fine with us," Kimball replied. He signaled to the others, and they slipped into the small darkened room of the house. With the exception of the small sleeping room at one side for Lucca and his wife and an equally small room at the other for the three children, there was no more. The main room served as kitchen, dining room and sitting room.

"Please to keep your voices down," Lucca pleaded. "Both my wife and kids sleep good, and I would just as soon they not see you."

"Fine," Ed said in a whisper. "First, good friend, some food, please."

Moving carefully in the dark, the farmer found bread, cheese and a jug of wine. Silently, the trio ate the small offering.

When they had finished, Kimball motioned to the farmer to follow him out the door. When they were out of earshot of the house, Kimball asked about the search.

"They have been up and down the valley, Eduardo. They found your parachutes, and they are offering a reward to anyone who turns you in. Also death for anyone who helps you. I am all that is left, Eduardo," he said pleadingly. "It's not just myself I worry about. If they find I have let you stay here, they will not only kill me but my wife and children as well. Why are you here, Eduardo?"

"Have no fear, old friend," Kimball said. "No one will ever know we have been here. We have a job to do, south of here. And I'm going to need some help. What do you know of any of our people, say around Biella, who might help?"

The farmer was silent for a moment. "These have been bad times, Eduardo. The Gestapo is everywhere now that Aosta has become a headquarters. So many of the old

66

fighters are gone, dead or in prison. I just don't know who's left. To tell you the truth, I keep to myself now. I have paid for the priest to say a mass every day for those good friends of mine who died with their lips sealed about me. It was too close, Eduardo. Now I am out of it."

"And for good reason, Lucca," Ed said soothingly, "but you must hear things. What about Guiseppe's unit? They were down by Ivrea, below Biella. Are they still active?"

The farmer shrugged. "It is possible. I have not heard that any of them were caught. But that does not mean that they are still active. I just don't know, Eduardo."

"In this business," Kimball replied, slapping the man on the back, "no news is good news. If you have not heard that Guiseppe has been taken, it must mean that he is still there. We will find him. Thank you. And now we need some sleep, just a couple of hours. It will still be dark when we leave."

Back in the house, Marco and Joelle had settled themselves on the wooden floor. Lucca nodded and whispered, "I shall get back in bed with my wife. I sleep lightly. I will awaken you in time."

He carefully entered the little side room and closed the door.

Kimball lay down and put his lips to Marco's ear. The American sat up and nodded. Silently, he picked up the submachine gun from the floor and slipped out the front door. Around the side of the house, he found a tree about fifteen yards from the building. He slouched down against the base of the tree, gun nestled in his lap, his eyes fixed on the small window to Lucca's bedroom. Three hours later, Kimball changed places with him.

It was four in the morning when the tall Canadian gently shook his sleeping team. In seconds, they collected their belongings and were out of the door. A dirt road went past the front of the farmhouse. At the gate, Kimball paused and then turned south, leading his team. Through the cracks of the front door, Lucca watched them go. Fifteen minutes later Kimball turned and moved west, back towards the wall of the valley. When they reached the trees above the cleared farmlands, he swung again, and the team moved north towards the Valpelline area where Cosimo had last been operating.

Lucca wrestled with himself until the sun was just edging over the eastern mountains. Then he dressed and left the house, walking down the dirt road to the bridge into Aosta.

An hour later he was standing, cap in hand, in front of Gestapo Major Conrad Koppfman. The Gestapo officer asked General Meirhausser to join them.

When Lucca was finished, the Germans knew Kimball's identity and that he was traveling with two others, one a small woman and another man. Lucca had not heard either of them talk, nor did he know their names. He emphasized that Kimball had questioned him closely about the partisan groups that might be working below Biella and that he had personally seen the trio set off to the south.

Within minutes, phone and radio messages were on their way to German units south of Aosta, turning the bulk of the searchers from the headquarters contingent in that direction.

As he was being dismissed, Lucca turned to Koppfman. "There was mention of a reward, Excellency," he said hesitatingly.

Koppfman glared at him. "If we find them, then there is time to talk of a reward. Meanwhile, be happy in the fact that you have done your duty to your country and your people. Out."

Riva was coming down the stairs as she saw Lucca leave the building. She drifted over to where Meirhausser was on the phone with the commander of the German units at Biella. He smiled up at her as she brushed the back of his blond hair with her hand.

"That's right, Colonel," Meirhausser shouted into the phone, "three enemy agents. One is a tall man, the other shorter and dark, and third is apparently a small woman. All dressed in American army work garb. Yes, that's right. And the tall one is the leader. A man by the name of Kimball, a Canadian. Our informant tells us that this Kimball is very familiar with the area from the years before the war."

Riva felt a great band constricting her chest, and for a moment she could not breathe. Her hand trembled on Meirhausser's head, and she pulled it away hurriedly.

"No, no, we don't know what their objective is, but it must be something down in your area. I want you to have every man you've got in this search. Post roadblocks. They must be caught. I know I can depend on you, Colonel. Heil Hitler." Meirhausser replaced the field phone, and again smiled up at Riva and took her hand.

"So lovely," he murmured. "Why have you been keeping yourself from me, *liebchen?*"

"But it hasn't been deliberate, Willi," she replied. "I just haven't been feeling well for several days. Nothing serious, just woman things."

Meirhausser patted her hand and nodded in understanding. "I eagerly await your full recovery," he said. "Did you ever hear of a Canadian by the name of Kimball who might have visited around here before the war?"

"Kimball, Kimball," Riva repeated with a thoughtful frown. "No, no, I can't say that I've ever heard the name before. What did he look like?"

Meirhausser smiled and shook his head. "It doesn't matter, beautiful one."

◆　◆　◆

The Proserpine team followed Mercury through the forest throughout the long day. Although they had said nothing to Lucca, each had three K-ration cartons in various flap pockets. They paused for lunch in the shelter of the trees

69

but still in sound of the river road. They could hear German vehicles moving from time to time, but most seemed to be going south. When they had finished eating, Marco used his sheath knife to dig a hole. They buried the remains of the cartons and tins, covered the hole and topped it with brush. Then they moved north again.

Twice during the day they had to change direction quickly to avoid search patrols crashing through the brush ahead, and once they had lain barely concealed near a small path as a patrol tramped by. The moment the last soldier had passed out of sight, they crept hurriedly across the dirt track and into the woods on the far side.

They were still moving north and slightly west at dusk, and Kimball urged them to a faster pace.

Joelle, wiry and almost as strong as either man for her size, was beginning to tire. Marco wordlessly took her submachine gun and slung it beside his on his shoulder. She smiled gratefully and hurried after the Canadian.

There was still faint light when Kimball led them at a fast pace down the mountainside towards the river. They could hear the water noisily churning below them. They came out of the forest and onto a massive boulder arched out over the river. Directly opposite was another, the outermost tips of both a scant six feet apart. Forty feet below, white water splashed among the rocks that had fallen in this narrow gorge.

"We cross here," Ed said, "but there is a problem. There's a gap that must be jumped, and I don't know if you can make it, Joelle. Perhaps we can find fallen timber to make some sort of a footbridge for you."

The little Frenchwoman walked to the edge of the rock and peered across the gap to the smooth surface of the boulder on the opposite bank. Then she looked down at the churning water and rocks below.

Out came the Gallic shrug.

She walked back to the two men.

"*C'est rien,* it's nothing," she said nonchalantly. "When I was a girl, I was what you call a Thomas boy, *non?*" She looked questioningly at the men.

"A tomboy," Vinnie laughed, "and I'll bet you were, too, Joelle."

"I was indeed," she said stoutly, "and I could jump much farther than that little crack."

"I don't know," Kimball hesitated, "I take to take . . . hey, for God's sake, no, Joelle."

Before he could finish his sentence, she raced for the edge of the rock. Both men held their breath as she sailed off the edge. The toe of her right boot just caught the edge of the opposite rock, tripping her and sending her sprawling on the hard surface. But she was across. She sat up and waved at them.

"Like I say," she shouted, "*c'est rien. C'est pour les enfants.*"

Marco looked at Kimball, and then they both broke out in laughter. Ed handed his submachine gun to the American.

"Toss all three over to me before you jump."

Minutes later, as the last light of the gray day vanished, they were again on the march, this time through the forest on the east side of the river.

Kimball called a halt at midnight for more food and two hours' rest. Joelle fell asleep on the pine needles even as she was eating. Again the two men alternated watch for an hour's sleep each.

At dawn, they were deep into the wild upper mountain country.

There had been no sign or sound of search parties throughout the night as they got deeper and deeper into the hills. An hour before, Kimball had found a faint path leading in the general direction of his intended route. It was worth taking a chance, and they made better time. There had been

71

no rain throughout the night, but a cold wind shivered the treetops. The clouds had blown away, and through the occasional breaks in the trees they could see the stars. Kimball had stopped from time to time to take compass readings.

There was a rosy glow on the eastern horizon, signaling at least the possibilities of a dry sunlit day. But the weather turned rapidly in the mountains. They would be grateful for a small part of a dry day.

They topped a small rise and then squeezed single file as the trail led into a narrow cleft in a huge ice-age boulder. Kimball was in the lead, with Joelle behind him. He was five paces into the cleft when two men sprang from either side of the front of the rock. Both were dressed in the worn patched garments of Italian mountain men, and they looked unkempt and wild. There was nothing shabby, however, about the pair of well-oiled and polished Thompson submachine guns aimed at Kimball's belly.

"What the hell!" Marco swung around, reaching for the grease gun on his shoulder. Another pair of Thompsons pointed at him from the upper end of the cleft, held by men who could have been blood brothers of the first pair. Joelle looked upwards and gave a little scream. Two more men flanked them from above on either side of the cleft.

Slowly, not to cause alarm, Kimball raised his empty hands and clasped them behind his neck. His companions followed suit.

"You will come out slowly," one of the men in front of the Canadian said in the heavy mountain accents of Italy, "one at a time. And keep your hands where they are."

Ed moved forward, one small step at a time. The men fell back, and Kimball felt an ice ball form in the pit of his stomach as one of them tightened his finger on the trigger.

It was still dark in the cleft of the rock, and the Proserpine team was in the shadows. The ambushers were standing in the first light of the rising sun.

Sinkingly, Kimball suddenly realized that none of these

72

men had ever seen the American olive-drab, almost grayish, fatigue uniform. In the dark of the shadows, it might look like the gray uniform of the Wehrmacht.

"Gently, my friends," Kimball said softly in his fluent Italian, an Italian that held traces of the mountain dialect from his many journeys to this part of Italy. "We are not Germans. We are friends. American, French and Canadian."

As he advanced, the pair continued to back away from him, the gun barrels never leaving his gut. He stepped out of the crevice in the rock into the early-morning light.

"*Alto!*"

Kimball stopped.

For a long minute, the taller of the two mountain men studied him.

"Take off your hat."

Keeping one hand still on his neck, Ed carefully and slowly pulled the black wool seaman's cap from his head. The light shone on his reddish-brown hair.

The other man looked at him for another full minute and then, with a sigh, lowered his gun.

"I know this one," he announced. "He has been here before."

The other five let their gun barrels sink as the taller man, obviously the leader of the patrol, slung his weapon and came to where Ed stood.

The Italian thrust out his hand. "I am Marcello," he said with a slight smile. "I remember your face, but I do not remember your name."

Ed broke into a broad grin and took the proffered hand. "I am Eduardo, and now I too remember your face."

"Ah, of course, Eduardo. You who gave us the guns and the will to fight. A good friend."

With that Marcello embraced the tall Canadian, and the others of the partisan group broke into laughter and crowded around.

Kimball quickly introduced Marco and Joelle. The partisans were impressed by an American who looked Italian and spoke a fair brand of the language, although his accent was harsh and unfamiliar to the ear.

"Aha," one of the six men cried, "I bet you are from New York. That's why you talk so funny. I have an uncle who lives there, and when he came home, he talked funny just like you."

Marco laughed and admitted he was from the most famous city in the world to immigrating Italians.

The entire group moved to the side of the trail, and wineskins and cheese quickly came out of pockets and pouches, while the Proserpine team produced the last of their K-rations.

Marcello was letting a stream of wine run into his mouth from his wineskin when he suddenly choked and sputtered, trying to talk while drinking. "But, of course, you must be the three spies we heard were dropped near Aosta three nights ago."

The three nodded.

Marcello made a mouth. "Then you have made very good time, my friends, to have traveled so far and to have eluded the Germans. You, Eduardo, are truly a good mountain man. But what do you seek in our hills?"

"I seek Cosimo," Kimball said simply.

There was immediate silence as the mountain men looked at each other.

"What do you want with Cosimo?" Marcello asked cautiously.

"I would speak with him about business," the Canadian replied.

Again there was silence.

"What business?"

Kimball looked at the rugged powerful man carefully. "You are not Cosimo, my friend."

Marcello's face clouded with anger, and he jerked upright.

"Does a man who wishes to talk private business with another man, one who was his friend, first have to tell the man's brother what the private affair might be?" Kimball asked.

Marcello thought about the statement for a moment and then grudgingly nodded his head.

"Such is true, and you were a friend of Cosimo's, though God in His heaven knows that today Cosimo has few friends. Nevertheless, we will take you to him."

In moments the food had been tucked away and the group was ready to move.

Before they started Marcello stood before Kimball, his hand outstretched. "First, your gun, signor, and those of your companions."

"Is this also the way one treats old friends?" Kimball asked angrily.

Marcello shrugged. "These are troubled times, and yesterday's friend is not always one today. If you are truly still Cosimo's friend, then you will get back your guns. Now, please," he demanded, shaking his outstretched hand.

"And suppose we run into a German patrol?" Ed asked. "They are looking for us. Are we to be defenseless?"

"The only Germans in these hills," one of the others said, sweeping his hand around the wild rocky mountainside, "are dead Germans."

Now it was Kimball who shrugged as he slipped the grease gun from his shoulder. Silently, he handed it to Marcello. Joelle and Marco did the same.

They moved out up the trail. Walking along behind Joelle, Marco once again felt the deep emotions of love and hate tearing at his gut. He was actually going to be face to face with that bastard who had deserted them. His hands shook with anger as he fought to bring himself under control. Kill him on sight. No, he must know without a shadow of a doubt who I am. Then kill him.

But what of the mission? Fuck the mission. And a lot

of GIs die because of it. So what, they die every day, that's what they get paid for.

Marco scarcely noticed that they were climbing higher and higher into the mountains. They had left the little path an hour before and had been working their way upward over unmarked rockfalls and through thinning timber.

Kimball sniffed and caught the scent of burning wood. Moments later, Marcello led them out of the woods and into a small clearing lying at the base of a mountain. Dotting the face of the cliff on a level with the small clearing was a series of caves.

A fire smoldered near the entrance to the largest of the openings, and another mountain man squatted beside it, stirring a smoke-blackened pot. He looked up when Marcello emerged from the trees and then jumped to his feet when he saw the Proserpine team. He dropped the wooden stick he had been using to stir and ran into the cave.

Marcello led them across the clearing as Cosimo walked out into the sunlight.

Marco gasped and shuddered at his first sight of his father.

He was a monstrously big man, as tall as Kimball but huge of chest and girth. Corded muscles rippled under rolled-up shirtsleeves, and his massive thighs seemed ready to burst out of the simple peasant trousers.

But it was his face that caught and held the trio. A heavy drooping mustache partially covered a livid scar that ran from the corner of his right eye across his cheek and vanished beneath the collarless ring of his shirt. There were deep pockmarklike scars on both cheeks, the reminders of a German bullet that had penetrated his face and exited out the other side.

He stood and surveyed the trio, scowling heavily.

Suddenly the scarred and savage face lighted with laughter, and he leaped forward.

76

"Eduardo, Eduardo," he roared and seized the tall Canadian in a rib-crushing *abbriccio.* "You have returned, you bastard. Oh, it is good to see you, old friend."

Now all of the partisans were laughing and smiling.

Wordlessly, Marco held out his hand to Marcello.

The partisan looked at the American for a second, and then shrugged and handed over the three M-3 submachine guns.

Cosimo released Ed from the bear hug but still held him in huge ham-sized hands, looking him up and down.

"You look good, my friend," he said, "but older, tired and maybe a little skinny."

"It's been a long war, Cosimo," Ed said.

"These are the three who parachuted near Aosta," Marcello reported. "We found them on the trail at the split rock. Eduardo said he came looking for you."

"I am glad you have come, Eduardo," Cosimo said, "but you have come at a bad time. Things are very poor for us here in the hills. This damned weather has kept our supply planes out on every scheduled drop day for a month.

"And the Germans and Fascist bastards have been all over. But enough of that. Tell me who your friends are." He turned and smiled at the Frenchwoman and the scowling Marco.

"*Momento,*" Kimball said in a low voice and grasped Cosimo by the arm. He led the huge man away from the others. "There is something you must know, old friend, before I introduce you to my companions. You and I both know that we have been through some tough fights together, and we have been friends for many years. Now I may be bringing trouble into your life, and for that I must first apologize. It is necessary."

Cosimo frowned puzzledly. "Trouble, Eduardo?" he asked. "Why, you have never brought me anything but trouble. But it has been the kind of trouble Cosimo likes. Trouble with Germans. Trouble with Fascists. You know nothing but trouble, my friend."

"This is a different kind of trouble, Cosimo, one that you can't fight. On the other hand, it may not be trouble, but joy. I don't know. But it is here, and you must know."

He told the partisan leader of the American check on his background. Then he dropped his bomb.

"The American soldier," he indicated Vinnie with his chin, "a good man, a good soldier, Cosimo. He is also your son."

The huge man was speechless. Slowly he turned and stared at Marco who glared icily back at him.

"You are sure of this, Eduardo?" Cosimo asked without dropping his eyes from the younger man's gaze.

Kimball nodded.

"So," Cosimo said slowly, "at last my crimes come home."

"No, you're wrong," Kimball said softly but urgently. "There is no crime. You did what you had to do. The boy knows the whole story. Now he is here. No, Cosimo, not crime."

"You do not know the whole story," Cosimo said. "Perhaps later."

He turned and walked straight to Marco and stood in front of him. Neither father nor son smiled. Silently, they stared at each other, neither having the will to speak the first word. A long minute passed.

Then Cosimo drew his long-bladed hunting knife from the sheath at the back of his belt. In a single motion, he handed the knife to his son, handle first, and ripped his own shirt down the front, baring his scarred chest.

"You may kill me," he said quietly. "You have my permission."

Vinnie's fist closed on the handle, and he turned his palm upwards in the fashion of a true knife fighter. His knuckles began to whiten in the tight grip on the knife. His eyes never left his father's face.

Then he turned suddenly and threw the knife at Cosimo's feet and walked away, his back stiff, his face as cold as a Rodin statue.

The partisan looked at the boy's back, then reached down and picked up the knife and slid it back into its sheath.

"Perhaps another day," he sighed and pulled up his shoulders. He turned and gave Joelle a courtly bow.

"I am Cosimo, signorina, and I bid you welcome. It is time that my daughter again had the company of another woman."

Now it was Kimball's turn to be speechless.

From the mouth of the cave a pretty teenaged girl emerged into the sunlight. Cosimo gently took Joelle by the arm and began leading her towards the girl. He paused and spoke over his shoulder. "Vincente," he called, "come and meet your sister."

Marco spun around, and his mouth dropped open at the sight of the girl. He whipped around and glared at Kimball.

The Canadian merely shrugged his shoulders. "This is as much of a surprise to me as it is to you," he said, walking over to the younger man. He shoved Marco gently in the direction of the caves. "Come on, Vinnie. Who knows how many other surprises this day holds? Right now, I'm damned proud of you."

Marco glowed despite himself.

◆　　◆　　◆

Cosimo—Angelo DeMarco—had never really been in love with his son's mother. It had been one of the traditional matches arranged by the families, in this case, DeMarco's eldest brother, who had immigrated to America years earlier and was by that time an American citizen, a well-to-do and prominent member of New York's Little Italy neighborhood and society.

79

Nonetheless, when DeMarco fled the United States after the bar killing, he fully intended to send for his wife and son as soon as he had the money to do so. But the Great Depression struck, and that money was never obtained. He was afraid to write his wife for fear of leading police to his whereabouts. But he knew that his brother would surely provide for his wife and son.

Back home in his mountain country, he found work with a small farmer, earning not much more than his keep and a place to sleep. But he also fell deeply in love, for the first time in his life, with the farmer's daughter. The farmer liked the big willing worker and saw in him the son he never had. So Angelo DeMarco turned his back on his past—a past he could never possibly return to—and illegally married again.

From that moment, his life became a mixture of guilt, happiness and sorrow—guilt for the lie he was living and for the wife and son in America, happiness with his farmer's daughter and later his own daughter, and finally, a year ago, tragedy.

He was away from the farm which the old man had willed to him, leading his partisans in an attack on a German ammunition train. During his absence, his wife was seized by the Germans, one of a group of random hostages taken in reprisal for an insult to a German officer. She was executed the same day.

The girl, Adriana, was saved only by the fact that she was visiting a girl friend on an adjoining farm and hadn't accompanied her mother to the town market that morning.

It all came out in the long hours of the day and into the night in the caves.

Throughout the rambling confession, broken by times to eat with the nine men who were the tough veteran survivors of Cosimo's original partisan group, Marco found himself automatically sitting beside his half-sister. He seemed both enthralled and stunned by the discovery of her.

"And that, Eduardo," Cosimo said with a huge sigh, "is the whole story, the part you never knew. I was afraid to tell you that I had a family here, maybe because of my own guilt. I don't know. But that's why we always met, even the first time, somewhere other than my home. But enough of this; I have much to go to confession for, perhaps too much. God will never forgive me."

He gazed across the cave at Marco and the girl.

"They look like good kids should," Cosimo concluded. "But why are you here, Eduardo? Why did you seek out Cosimo? Was it only to bring the boy?"

Kimball shook his head and then began outlining the mission the team had been given. When he finished, Cosimo shook his head.

"Too late, Eduardo," he said. "Look around you. How many do you see? We are all that are left."

"This is not a job for more men," Ed insisted; "it is a job for good and trained men."

"No, my old friend, I cannot ask them to risk themselves on such a mission. It is too late."

Kimball sighed and then started to rise. "So be it, Cosimo. Then this must be our last good-bye. For if you won't help, we will still try it ourselves, we three. The job must be tried, even if we fail."

Cosimo reached out a great hand and grasped Kimball by the shoulder, pushing him back to the ground. "Not so fast, Eduardo, perhaps there is a way." He thought for several minutes. "Tell me again how you plan to get out of Italy."

Kimball sketched his ideas.

Cosimo thought further. "It might work. It just might work." He turned to the Canadian. "I will enter into a bargain with you, Eduardo, old friend."

"Every time I've entered into a bargain with you," Kimball smiled, "I found out I was not only paying full price but double price. But what is your bargain?"

"No, no, not that kind of bargain. We will help you under one condition," Cosimo said. "If you get out of the castle alive and are still able to try for the Swiss border, Adriana goes with you. I must get her out of here," he added in a low voice. "It's just a matter of time before the Gestapo get to us. I want her safe, and I want her in the hands of someone who will look after her, perhaps get her to America with my other family. That, Eduardo, is my bargain."

Kimball looked across at the girl chattering happily with her half-brother on one side and Joelle on the other. All three were laughing. The girl could be waiting outside the castle. If they made it, it would be worth the try. If they didn't, there would be at least two of the partisans with her to help her escape.

He held out his hand to Cosimo. "Done."

The big man roared with pleasure and almost knocked Kimball sprawling with a great thump on the back. "Now," he roared, "we make plans. But first I must tell my people."

Within minutes, all nine of the partisans were crowded into the main cave along with those already there. Wine bottles, many wine bottles, seemed to appear out of the air and were passed from hand to mouth to hand as the partisans crowded around the cleared space on the floor where Ed had spread his silk-cloth reproductions of the castle layout, Joelle's cave map and a map of the area.

"First, friend Eduardo," Cosimo said, "show me where you think you hid your drop bundles."

Kimball found the two peaks on the map that he had taken his sightings on the night of the drop. He consulted a small notebook where he had recorded the azimuth readings, then laid the compass on the map and drew bearing lines along his recorded figures. The lines intersected at a point about five miles northwest of Aosta.

"And where, signorina," Cosimo asked of Joelle, "is the entrance to your cave?"

Unhesitatingly, she pointed to a place on the map four miles east of Aosta.

"That means that those four bags have to be hauled from their hiding place across the river, around Aosta and up to the cave entrance," Ed remarked.

"That is merely a detail," Cosimo replied.

"That may be just a detail to you, but how the hell do we get four fifty-pound bundles across that river? Just walk up to the sentry box at the bridge and tell them we're delivering laundry to the castle?"

"We get them across just the way you crossed, Eduardo. At the rock bridge."

"But that's at least five miles upstream and north of the castle."

"So we go five miles upstream north of the castle to the rock bridge and cross there," Cosimo said with finality. "It is no big thing. Then we work our way across this slope and down to the entrance to the signorina's cave."

"Those bundles are damned big and bulky, Cosimo," Ed complained.

"You are not thinking, old friend," the partisan chief said. "Not counting the ladies, we will be twelve big strong men. Who says we carry four fifty-pound cowlike bundles? When we leave here in the morning, each of us will have a packsack. We picked them up from the graycoats during one of our train raids. Even a simple peasant like myself can figure out that that comes out to less than twenty pounds per man. Like I said, nothing."

Kimball smiled in admiration. "You're quite right. I should have known better, Cosimo," he said. "We should be back at the drop packs in two nights. It took us three to get here, but we were dodging German patrols, and I think most of them have been withdrawn to the . . ."

"Two nights," Cosimo broke in with disgust. "What do you expect us to do? Crawl there on our hands and knees? We will be there after dark tomorrow night."

"How in hell are you going to manage that?"

"Show me how you got here," Cosimo demanded.

Ed picked out their route on the map.

The big partisan roared with laughter.

"You wander like a cow looking for water. These are Cosimo's mountains. I will show you a new trail that will make your heart beat faster, but we'll be there tomorrow night. And early enough to move everything to the cave entrance before the light of the next day."

They left at dawn, each of the partisans loaded down with as much ammunition as he could carry, all armed with Thompsons and an assortment of knives. Wine, cheese and dried meat were stuffed into bulging pockets.

In the chill late-October air, Cosimo led them out and up from the caves, climbing steadily into the mountains but always moving slightly to the south.

Adriana, who had been born in the mountains and even traveled this trail, came along easily. The hardy Frenchwoman, who had climbed cave walls and mountainsides all of her life, pushed hard on the heels of the partisan in front of her.

Cosimo called a halt at midday. "Eat something," he ordered. "There will be no further chance until we come back down into the forest at dark."

Ahead of them appeared to be the sheer rock wall of the mountain. With two of Cosimo's men leading the way, the party edged out onto a rock ledge, at places less than eighteen inches wide. On their right hand was the bare rock wall. To their left, three thousand feet of nothingness.

"Jesus Christ," Marco muttered as he edged his way along the ledge, his palms damp with sweat and his heart pounding. This was no place for a New York boy to be. He glanced ahead and saw the huge bulk of his father surefooting along the ledge like a great mountain goat. The young American gritted his teeth and kept moving.

The ledge, partially blocked in places by rockfalls they had to scramble over, went on for nearly two miles. Then they were off the rock and onto a steep but grassy slope with the forest a quarter of a mile ahead. The two miles on the ledge had cut twenty miles from Kimball's original way north.

Cosimo called a brief halt at the edge of the trees. He conferred briefly with four of his men, and then they melted away on both sides into the trees. Cosimo gave them time to get ahead and then signaled the others to follow him. Cosimo had his "point" out.

Clouds were again settling over the mountains, and the sun had vanished shortly after they had come off the ledge. A light rain was falling through the pine forest.

Just as dark was settling over the mountains, the partisan leader called another halt. As the group sank to the ground, he put his hands to his lips and issued a strange muffled whistling sound.

Three minutes later the four men on the point drifted out of the trees and joined them.

"Now we eat again," Cosimo said. "But no lights. And if you ladies will forgive me, it is also the time for necessary personal relief. We men will remain here and prepare the food while the ladies go."

Adriana giggled and rose.

"Thank God," Joelle murmured as she hurried into the dark privacy of the trees.

An hour later, in a pitch-dark rain-filled night, Cosimo unerringly led them into the small clearing where the Proserpine team had landed. A few moments' search by Kimball and Joelle, and the bundles were uncovered.

Quickly, the contents of the bags were divided up

among the empty packsacks that each carried. At the last moment, Cosimo changed his mind. Four of the packs were emptied and distributed among the remaining eight.

"Another five pounds is nothing," he said. "I want the four men on the point to be able to move fast and easily if they have to."

In less than a half hour, they were once again on the move, the point spread across the front of the little column. Even going back to the rock bridge that Kimball had led them over four days earlier took less time on another trail that Cosimo knew.

When they reached the gap in the rocks, it was raining and in deep darkness. Only the sound of the rushing water below was evidence of the river.

This time Kimball insisted on protection. One of the coils of nylon climbing rope came out of the packs. Cosimo scoffed at the rope and pointed across the gap. The four point men were already across and standing there, waiting for them.

"I don't give a damn," Ed said firmly. "This rock is slippery, and that's all it would take on a night like this."

The end of the nylon was heaved across the gap and anchored by the men on the other side around a nearby tree trunk. Then each of the packs was slipped by its harness straps onto the rope, and, one by one, slid down the inclined rope to the far side.

When the equipment was across, the loose end of the rope was secured to Joelle's waist.

She smiled at the rope and then ran like a deer for the edge. This time she landed in the dark and skidded to a slippery halt in the arms of one of the waiting partisans.

Adriana followed her, and then the remaining men.

It was at exactly four-thirty in the morning in a wind-driven rain that the reinforced Proserpine team came in out of the wet into the dark dry air of Joelle's cave system.

86

Brush was pulled back over the narrow entrance to the cave and two of the partisans posted as guards.

Using one of the dozen miners' lamps they had packed, Joelle led them fifty feet into the cave and into a large dry chamber. It was time to sleep.

◆ ◆ ◆

The cloud cover had again dropped almost to the valley floor, and the rain continued. From her bedroom window, Riva could see no farther than the tall ornamental iron fence surrounding the immediate castle grounds. And the rain continued to fall.

The damp coldness of the room matched her own chill fear as she sat and looked out into the gray morning. It was now five days since Eduardo had been dropped onto the mountain slope, and yet there had been no sign that he was coming to the castle. But it had to be the plans—and herself—that drew him here. Of all the S.O.E. field agents, he was the one most capable of operating in these mountains. He knew she was here and probably knew that she had shared Willi's bed. What would he think of her? She shivered from the cold that penetrated the room and the even icier grip within.

She allowed her thoughts to drift back to the wonderful month in Saint Moritz nearly eight years before. Would all of this have been different if Eduardo had even hinted at marriage? He had been a warm, tender and considerate lover and great fun to be with in all things. But neither of them seemed to want to consider the possibility of a longer union. It was as though they both deliberately kept conversation away from marriage, although the word "love" had been on both of their lips many times, in gay happy parties with their ski companions and in the wild passionate moments in bed together.

It had been sweet and just a little tearful at the end, but she quickly fell back into her family life when she returned to Italy. Then there had been dear, wonderful and romantic Milo, who brought out in her new dimensions of the word "love" and who swept her up in almost medieval gallantry and chivalry. Even later when Eduardo came to visit, she felt no regrets at her marriage. Kimball, as both friend and gentleman, never presumed or hinted at their earlier intimacies. Ah, what good friends he and Milo became. But old loves die hard.

Stop this, you silly goose, she prodded her inner self. But the mood for introspection was too strong.

How lucky she had been that all three men in her life were so different in backgrounds and temperament, yet so alike in their emotional and physical attractions. Even Willi, tall handsome Willi, whom she was betraying.

From the moment he entered the castle more than two years before, she had felt strong physical attraction to him. When it became obvious in a very short time that he was not just another Nazi street thug, but, rather, a gentleman of breeding and education, and kind and warm, the attraction grew even stronger.

When instructions came from S.O.E. to become closer to him in order to be privy to information she could supply to the Allies, she had never had a moment of physical revulsion. A young passionate woman needs a man, and it was with racing pulse and warm wet thighs that she went to his bed for the first time. Poor sweet Willi. Born on the wrong side of chivalry.

Now she was sitting like a lovesick puppy, staring out a gray bleak window and waiting for an old love to rescue her like some maiden in a fairy tale.

Riva shook her head angrily at herself and left the room.

In his office beneath Riva's feet, Meirhausser had Koppfman across the desk from him.

"It's been five days now since they landed," the general growled, "and not one damn word other than that single report from the farmer. What the hell's the matter with the Gestapo, Major?"

The hatchet-faced Gestapo officer angrily exhaled a cloud of cigarette smoke.

"And I might ask the same question, Herr General," Koppfman retorted. "What the hell's the matter with the Wehrmacht and those pretty boys in their tight uniforms, your cute Waffen SS? You've not even crossed their path with all your searching."

"If we didn't find them within the first twenty-four hours, Koppfman, it means only one thing to me. They have gone underground and are being assisted by the partisans. You, Major, are the one who has been bragging around here about how effectively you have crushed the resistance. Well, I suggest to you, and am considering suggesting it to Berlin, that you have been far from effective, not only in stamping out the underground but in your inability for these past five days to come up with a single sighting from your so-called vast network of informants." Meirhausser paused to bring his temper under control. "This is a Gestapo matter, Major. Uniformed combat troops are not the tools you use to burrow into a rabbit warren. You send in a weasel."

Koppfman flushed with anger and ground out his cigarette in the ashtray on Meirhausser's desk.

"We will find them, Herr General, if I have to take every Italian in these hills and shoot them one at a time—after I cut off their hands."

"You had better," Meirhausser said ominously. "Not only have you not found them, you haven't the slightest notion of why they came in the first place. I cannot believe that there is not some connection with this headquarters. I don't believe their landing so close to Aosta was accidental, and now I'm beginning to believe that that peasant who came to see you was just dragging a dead fish across their trail. There hasn't been a hint of them south of here. I want you to redouble your efforts, especially in and around the town. It is imperative that we find them and learn what they are after.

"There is some good news for a change, however. This morning I was informed by Feldmarshal Kesselring's headquarters in Milan that the Allied offensive has been stopped short of the Po River. And with this weather continuing and winter not far away, there seems little chance that they will launch another major offensive until spring. So we have bought some time, Koppfman, time we desperately need to complete work on Project Guardian, already behind schedule. Find them, Koppfman, find them!"

◆　　　◆　　　◆

Gray light was filtering into the cave, both from the narrow entrance and from small blowholes in the dome, as the Proserpine team prepared for the final assault on Vulcano Castle.

Adriana and three of Cosimo's men were to remain in the main cavern near the entrance until the others had broken into the castle's underground system. Then would begin the second stage of the plan.

Madame Gaussin had her drawings laid out on the floor and was talking with Kimball, Marco and Cosimo. During the past twenty-four hours, a subtle change had taken place within the young American. Although he exchanged as few words as possible with his father, nonetheless there was a noticeable softening of his stiff angry attitude. Watching the huge partisan move fearlessly across the cliff face, observing his positive leadership and ability with his men and his high degree of common-sense strategy, Marco unconsciously showed grudging admiration for the man he had hated for so long.

As Joelle was giving her briefing to the leaders, the other members of the partisan team to accompany them into the caves were separating unneeded items from their packs. The plan called for the team to penetrate the cave system to a point under one of the castle's underground accesses and to make an entry hole. Then they would return to the cave entrance and prepare for the second phase of the assault. The German Army uniforms, forged papers, gas masks, tear-gas canisters and a few other items were set aside. For this part of the venture, they would be carrying only the explosive charges, crowbars and mountain axes to clear their way through rubble and rock.

"We are here," the Frenchwoman said, pointing to the drawings. "We go in this direction. The first two miles are *très facile.* There are a couple of narrow openings we might have to widen to get this great bull through," she grinned at Cosimo, "since he is twice the girth of both Jacques and myself. We managed it quite easily."

The three men followed her moving finger.

"Then we come to this passage," she said, "and our work begins. I have been into it for more than a mile, but not to the end. But even where I turned back, we should be most close to either this underground storage vault," she pointed to the drawings of the castle works lying beside her, "or to this old escape tunnel. It would be better, I think, if we can get another hundred yards or more into the passageway. I estimate it should be about under a mile to this very narrow passage. There were numerous rockfalls, even when I was here eight years ago. I have no idea what the condition of the passageway is today. And I could proceed no further than I did because of a very great fall which blocked the entire channel."

"How long do you think it will take us to get to the point where we can start cutting up into the castle system?" Marco asked.

"That is for *Le Bon Dieu* to say, *mon ami. Avec bonne chance,* with good luck, one, perhaps two days. With heavy rockfalls or possibly even cave-ins, much longer. This I do know," she said, "when we reach the point I estimate to be under the vault, we should be less than thirty feet below the floor."

"OK," Ed said, rising and lifting his packsack from the floor, "let's get on with it."

In moments, the nine pack-laden men were following the slight figure of Joelle into the back of the main cavern and into a low passage leading west. Five of the party, including Joelle in the lead, were wearing carbide miners' lamps strapped to their heads. All carried hand torches but had been warned by both Kimball and Cosimo to use them sparingly to conserve batteries.

Joelle's yellow light danced and moved across the dark rock walls of the passage. All ten were stooped to avoid the low ceiling, and Cosimo was on his hands and knees, dragging his pack with one hand.

The passage quickly widened into another smaller cavern high enough to stand erect.

Madame Gaussin consulted briefly with her drawings and then led the file of men into another opening at the far side, this large enough to walk through comfortably. Marco, his pack containing the extra miners' lamps, some food, the coils of rope and the detonators, was directly behind Joelle. Cosimo was in the middle of the file, and Ed brought up the rear. They moved steadily through the series of smaller caverns and tunnels, deeper into the mountain. Once they were stopped by what appeared to be a recent rockfall. Joelle moved back out of the way, and Marco and two of the partisans pried and heaved to move the loose rubble away. In ten minutes the tunnel was again wide enough for crawl space over the small rockfall.

It took them two hours to reach the small cavern from which the final passage would begin.

Joelle gathered the team around her. "Now we enter the

most difficult section," she said. "Let us rest here for a few minutes and then go in. From this point we will be crawling, for it is quite low and, in places, most narrow."

"Does this thing have any side exits where you might make the wrong turn?" Marco asked.

"No, why?"

"Then let me lead the way," the young American said. "When we hit a cave-in, I'll be in position to set charges. If it's as narrow as you say, I might not be able to squeeze past you."

"You are going to set the charges?" Cosimo asked incredulously.

Marco's eyes bored into his father's. "Yes, me, old man. That's what I do for a living when I'm not wearing this soldier suit. Any other questions?"

Cosimo's eyebrows shot up, and he made a face and shook his head. So much he didn't know about this boy. And a man who works with high explosives. More new conceptions of his recently found son were blossoming.

"But I am the one who has brought you here," Joelle protested. "I should be in front."

"Marco's right, Joelle. If the passage is as you say, he can't make a wrong turn. If he runs into something that needs explanation, he can call back to you. His idea makes sense."

Kimball and several of the others had lighted up cigarettes as they sat with their backs against the rock wall of the small cave.

"Joelle," Ed called out, "this smoke is rising, and I can see it swirling a little up there. What's the air situation down here? It still seems fresh, although damp and musty."

"There are many small airholes throughout the system," she said. "Most of them are invisible to the eye. This is basically a limestone matrix, and it is honeycombed, I think that is the word, with holes and pockets like a great

93

piece of cheese. The air is good. However, it is not this good in the small places such as we will be entering."

"In that case," Vinnie cut in, "I don't want all of us going in there at one time."

"What do you mean?" Kimball asked.

"Look, if we hit a fall, I have to blow it out," Marco explained. "That's a straight one-man job. But before I can set the charge, everyone behind me is going to have to back up a helluva long way before it blows. That takes time. It doesn't make sense for all ten of us to be in there at one time. I'll take you and Ricardo here," he indicated the partisan at his side, "and Joelle. You two are both carrying the nitro-starch. Bring the crowbars along. The rest of you stay here until we get to the point where we can go up."

"There is another cave, just about this size," Joelle said, "which would be not too far from where we will try to make our way upwards. If you can get us there, Vincente, then the rest can join us."

"Fine."

"And what if you run into something too big for you to clear?" Cosimo asked.

"I've never found one yet, old man," Marco said evenly. Cosimo flushed. "But if I do, I'll call you for help."

The working party moved to the narrow tunnel. Kimball turned. "One thing, Cosimo. I suggest you turn off the lights and save on the carbide. This is all we have. I don't think you need light just to sit here."

Cosimo nodded and reached for his own lamp. One of the partisans remaining with him looked at him nervously.

"What's the matter, G'vanni? Afraid of the dark? Don't you worry, little boy. Cosimo will keep you safe."

The man flushed and uttered an obscenity in Italian. Cosimo laughed, and the lights died.

On their hands and knees, the small team entered the tunnel with Marco leading the way. For the slight Joelle there was no problem, but for the larger men it was a tight fit.

They were less than two hundred yards into the passageway before Marco's light reflected off broken rock from floor to ceiling.

The American studied the fall for a couple of seconds, then pushed his pack to one side and rolled over on his back. He reached up and picked up a large block of rock and carried it down his body. Roberto had already caught on and was on his back to pass it to Kimball.

The Canadian took one look at the size of the rock and then yelled back down the tunnel for Cosimo. In moments the lamp on the big partisan's head came down the tunnel.

"Something we didn't think about, Cosimo," Ed said. "We've got to get the rock out of the passage and put it somewhere. I saw a side hole a few yards back. Some of it can go in there. But we may have to handle it all the way back to the cave. Joelle, these are going to be just too heavy for you to lift. You back out with Cosimo. If we run into a problem, we'll send for you. Cosimo, get the rest of your men and start passing this stuff down to that hole. Put it anywhere you can get it out of the way."

"But how will you know when you have reached the proper point to turn upwards?" the Frenchwoman protested.

"You said there's another cavern ahead. We'll stop when we get there, and you all can join us then."

The narrow passageway rumbled and echoed with the sound of stone banging against stone as each rock was passed down the line. Finally, only one large boulder remained, not filling the passageway but not leaving room enough for a person to squeeze through.

Marco rolled onto his stomach and looked over the opening above the rock. His light faded out in the open gloom ahead.

"Time for the first bang," he said. He studied the rock.

"Hand me three blocks, Roberto," he ordered. "All the rest of you back out. Get past that last turn we came around."

As the others inched their way back down the passage, Vinnie pulled a detonator and fuse from his own pack, along with a large roll of tape.

In moments he had the blocks draped and taped around the boulder.

"Everybody back?" he called. Kimball's muffled assent came.

Marco cut the fuse and placed it. He closed his pack and seized the harness straps. Then he lit the fuse and began a furious backwards crawl down the passageway, dragging the pack with him. The fuse was glowing brightly as he backed around the corner.

"Hold your ears," he called and clapped his hands over his own.

Fifteen seconds later the charge went off like a shell in a cannon, sending billowing clouds of dust and smoke rolling down the narrow passage along with a hail of small chips. Despite his warning, the four were virtually deafened by the blast. They lay there until the thick dust began to settle, and then Marco crawled forward. The boulder lay shattered in small pieces, and the passage was open. He brushed some of the rubble to one side and crawled through.

"It's open," he yelled, "let's go."

Slowly and painfully, the party inched its way along the passage. Three times the passage was blocked so badly that Marco was forced to blow their way through. The final charge of the day was the worst. For more than a hundred yards back down the tunnel, there were neither turns nor potholes to deposit loose rock. All nine men were in the tunnel manhandling the stone out of the way.

When the others had cleared back down the tunnel, Marco set a long fuse and began the awkward backwards scuttling to reach the others. Suddenly his pack harness snagged on a jagged outcropping. Frantically, he inched back up to free the strap. The pack held all of their detonators. If he abandoned it, the impact of the charge coming down the cannon-barrel tube of the tunnel was sure to set them off.

Sweat and dirt rolled into his eyes as he fought to get the strap clear. Finally it pulled free, and he again hurried back down the tunnel. He glanced at his sweep-second hand and felt cold sweat break. There were less than ten seconds left on the fuse, and he hadn't reached the curve in the tunnel.

His head swept around, and the yellow beam of his miner's hat caught a shallow oblong depression in the tunnel wall. Unhesitatingly, he dragged the pack and flung it into the depression and then rolled in beside it, on his right side, his back to the face of the tunnel. There was no way to protect his left ear.

The massive roar of the explosion shook the tunnel.

Small jagged chunks of rock and smaller chips again came exploding down the tunnel in another cloud of dust and smoke. When the echoes of the blast had died away, Marco continued to lie on his side in the shallow niche in the wall. He was stunned and deafened, and his left eardrum had been blown in. So intense was the lancing pain in his head that he didn't feel the deep gouge in his back, ripped open by a piece of flying rock.

Roberto, scrambling back up the tunnel, was the first to find him. "Eduardo," he screamed. "It is Vincente. He's been hurt."

The partisan moved up the tunnel to let Kimball come even with the moaning body of the American sergeant. Blood was seeping through Marco's torn jacket. Ed ripped the rest of the jacket apart. He found a field first-aid kit in his pocket and swabbed away the welling blood. It appeared to be only a shallow wound. He sprinkled sulfa powder the length of the gouge and then held the dressing in place with one hand.

"Lie still, Vinnie," he said, "it's not deep. Let me slip my hand under you and get the other end of this dressing."

He secured the bandage and gently rolled Marco out of the depression and into the tunnel. The American's eyes were just beginning to focus. He stared up at Kimball and then blinked.

Ed smiled. "You OK?"

Marco frowned and looked at Kimball's lips. "Yeah," he muttered. "I think so. I can't hear a word you're saying, Ed, and my left ear hurts like hell. I think it blew out."

For the first time, Kimball noted the blood trickling from the engineer's ear.

Marco eased himself up onto his elbows and shook his head. "Jesus Christ, that was close," he said. "Goddamned pack hung up on a rock, and I couldn't get back in time." The ringing in his head was less intense, although his left ear still throbbed with pain. As if from a great distance, he heard Kimball speak.

"That's all for you, Vinnie. Let's get you out of here."

The chunky young Italian-American shook his head. "Forget it. I've had worse than this." He reached up and tapped Roberto on the leg and then rolled back into his depression. "Get the fuck outta the way, Roberto, and let me up there."

The Italian stared blankly at him.

Marco grinned and switched to Italian. The partisan moved back.

Marco rolled into the tunnel and grabbed the pack that had almost cost him his life. He moved up the tunnel to where the charge had been set. There was hardly any dust left in the tunnel, and the passage was open. Marco raised his head, and the beam of his lamp caught the last traces of the swirling smoke and dust being drawn up the tunnel ahead of him. In fifteen minutes, they had cleared enough of the debris for them to continue, and five minutes later, Marco crawled out of the passageway into the last cave.

When Kimball entered the cave behind Roberto, Marco was slumped against the wall, smoking a cigarette. The Canadian stood up and let his light play over the walls and ceiling of the cave. It was about fifteen feet high, nearly circular, and against the far wall water dripped down to pool on the floor before trickling into some cracks underfoot.

He looked at his watch. It had taken them ten hours to go just over a mile. It was time to stop. Marco was exhausted and in pain. It would take at least three hours to reach the mountain entrance to the cave, the large main cavern where Adriana and the others waited. There was no way Marco could make that trip.

He turned to Roberto and the other partisan who had followed them up the tunnel.

"Drop your packs and leave us what water or wine you have," he directed. "I'll stay here with Marco. Go back and tell Cosimo we've reached this cave. He and the others can either stay there for the night or go back to the main cave and then come back up here in the morning. Tell him that when they do come to bring extra water and food."

The two Italians nodded and dropped their packs to the floor. They unslung wineskins from their shoulders and handed them to him.

"Thanks," Ed grinned, "want a sip before you go?"

They both licked their lips and then looked at the exhausted and grimy Marco. They shook their heads and vanished back into the tunnel.

Kimball dragged the packs over to where Marco was slumped and handed him a wineskin. The American gratefully pulled on the strong red liquor.

"Ears any better?"

"Yeah, I'm beginning to hear all right with my right ear, but the left is gone and hurts like hell, and my head still rings a little. But I'm OK, otherwise. Just pooped."

"Good. Feel like eating something?"

Marco shook his head. "Not right now. Lemme rest a bit. Then I'll eat. What do we have?"

"What else?" Ed replied with a smile. "K-rations."

Kimball reached up, turned off his lamp and removed it from his head. He pulled a flashlight from his pack and tucked it into his jacket pocket. Marco's lamp was already out.

They were stretched out in the dark, only the glowing tips of their cigarettes indicating their presence, when they both saw the first faint light coming out of the tunnel.

The yellow glow grew brighter, and a few moments later, Joelle Gaussin crawled out of the tunnel, dragging a large wineskin and a water bottle behind her. Her pockets were bulging.

" 'allo, *mes amis,*" she called out cheerily in the direction of the glowing tips, "room service 'as arrived."

She caught them in the beam of her lamp and joined them. Joelle dropped the bottle and bag, and reached under her jacket to extract a huge candle tucked into her waistband. In seconds, its soft flickering light gave the damp cave the impression of a warm and intimate room.

"What the hell are you doing here, Joelle?" Ed demanded. "I gave orders for the others either to stay where they were or to go back to the entrance."

"And so they did, *chère* Ed," she said. "But I am not one of the 'others.' I am a charter member of the team, and this is where I belong. Are you sad that I have come?"

Marco laughed. "Joelle, you really are something else. If I were just a couple of years older . . ."

"Why, Sergeant," she replied coyly, "I am a married woman." She paused and then grinned at him. "Besides, what difference do a couple of years make?"

The men burst into laughter.

Joelle had managed to stuff virtually every edible among

Cosimo's men into her pockets. That was the principal reason the partisans had returned to the main cavern. They were hungry.

Several pulls on the wineskin and Marco felt rested enough to eat. Between the K-rations and the cheese, bread and other items Joelle had scrounged from the partisans, the three ate well.

When they had finished and cleaned up the remains, Kimball examined the wound in Marco's back.

It had stopped bleeding, although the dressing was dark and stiff with dried blood. Using the water Joelle had brought, the Canadian softened the stiff dressing and gently peeled it away. In the flickering candlelight, the wound appeared to be ugly but superficial.

"Oh, *le pauvre,*" Joelle exclaimed as she saw the deep gouge. She brushed her hand over Marco's head as Kimball applied fresh sulfa and a clean dressing.

The Canadian gave Marco the wineskin. "Take a few more swigs of that, Vinnie, then try and get some sleep," he said. "This is one night when we don't have to keep one eye open."

With one of the packs under his head for a pillow, Marco was asleep in five minutes.

When the sergeant was sleeping, Joelle slipped on her headlamp and stood up.

"Where are you going?" Ed asked.

"I want to take a look up the passageway. We are very close, *mon capitaine.*"

"I'll go with you."

Leaving the sleeping Vinnie, the two of them stooped and then crawled into the opening at the side of the small cave leading in the direction of the castle. This time Joelle was again leading the way. There was surprisingly little debris in the passage and no major rockfalls. About a quarter of a mile into the tunnel, the passageway took a sharp turn to the left, downhill and away from the castle. At the point it turned was another slightly smaller cave.

Joelle stood up and looked about. Then, ordering Kimball to wait for her, she crouched and entered the passage leading downhill. He could see the glow of her lamp for a dozen yards, and then it disappeared around a bend. Five minutes later she was back.

Stretching her neck, she played her light over the roof of the little cave. The ceiling nearly touched Kimball's head when he stood up and was not more than seven feet from the floor. She nodded with satisfaction.

"*C'est ici,*" she said with authority, "this is the place. We are now under the castle works."

"Excellent." Ed surveyed the roof of the cave. "I wonder just how much goddamned rock is up there between us and the tunnel or vault."

"As I said before," Joelle said, "I would extimate about thirty feet. But I also have a feeling that it may not be all solid rock. Look, *mon ami.*" She pointed to several small, round and smoothly eroded holes near the top of the dome. "I would hope that we are in a good porous limestone area. If such is so, then our work will be much easier."

Ed examined the holes. "I hope you're right. Come on, let's get back to Vinnie and get some sleep ourselves. It's going to be another long and tough day tomorrow."

◆ ◆ ◆

Wheezing and uttering a steady stream of oaths, Cosimo shoved his huge bulk through the narrow opening and into the cave where the trio had spent the night. His six partisans followed him into the chamber.

Their lamps picked out two packs lying against the wall near the entrance to the far passage, but the cave was deserted.

" 'Allo," he roared, his booming voice echoing off the walls, "where are you?"

Moments later, as if from a great distance, they heard a voice filtering down the far tunnel. Cosimo went to the entrance and stuck his head through the opening.

"Is this the right one?" he bellowed.

This time Kimball's voice was faint but distinct.

Signaling his men to follow him and dragging his pack, Cosimo sighed and went down on all fours for another crawling session. But just as he was starting up the passage, Kimball's voice came again, more clearly.

"Stay there. I'm coming back."

The massive partisan chief muttered a silent prayer of thanks and backed out of the opening. "Turn off those lights," he ordered his men.

Only Cosimo's lamp was burning as Ed emerged from the passageway. He stood up and stretched, then grinned at Cosimo.

"We're there, old friend," he said happily.

"You mean you're up into the castle already?"

"No, but Joelle says we're right under the proper spot. Vincente is up there now, deciding how best to get us through the roof of the small cave at the end of this passage. They should be back in a couple of minutes."

When the American and the woman returned, Kimball and Cosimo looked at them questioningly.

"I can blow it OK," Marco said. "The only thing that bothers me now is the noise. I set off blocks of starch and it's going to make one hell of a boom. They might hear it up there."

"I doubt it very much, Vinnie," Kimball said. "Those underground rooms haven't been used for years, maybe not for a couple of centuries. And they're damned deep under the castle itself. The main floor of the building is all stone and marble, and it's built like a rock quarry."

"There is another thing," Cosimo added. "There is a very great storm raging outside this morning. Very heavy rain and much thunder coming off the mountains. It was very loud when we left the entrance."

Marco digested the information. "OK, you're the boss, but I'm still gonna cut down on the size of the charges. I can always use a series of smaller ones, rather than one big boom. Besides, I don't want to bring down that whole ceiling at one time." He hunkered down and scratched lines in the dust of the cave floor.

"Joelle thinks we've got about thirty feet to go through. If she's right, the far end of this tunnel where it turns here," he indicated the spot on his drawing, "looks big enough to hold most of the garbage we'll be blowing down. I ain't got the least idea of how long it will take or how many charges. I set 'em. They blow, and we all go in there and start heaving rock. Then we go back and do it again. If we find the bottom of the vault without blowing a hole in it, no more nitrostarch. We use the bars and pry our way in. That way, we take no chances on someone hearing or feeling the stuff go off."

"This time," Kimball ordered, "you leave your pack here and just take the detonator and fuse with you. And make damned sure that the fuse is long enough. We're not in that much of a hurry that a couple of minutes are going to make any difference."

Marco stuffed a detonator and fuse in his pocket, along with his tape roll and a block of wet clay he extracted from his own pack. Followed by the faithful Roberto with the pack of explosive charges, he went back up the passage. The others waited.

Ten minutes later, Roberto was back.

They spent another anxious fifteen minutes before Marco came crawling out of the opening, a smile on his face. He shot a quick look at his watch. "Thirty seconds," he announced.

The muffled boom echoed into the cave exactly on the second. Moments later, with Marco in the lead and Kimball right behind him, the Proserpine team and the partisans went up the passageway. Packs were left behind in the chamber, but the heavy pry bars and mountain axes went along.

A huge pile of broken rock lay in the center of the small cave. Joelle examined the debris together with Marco.

"It is much limestone," she announced.

Cosimo looked at the pile and then turned to the others who had crowded into the smoky dusty space.

"All right, let's get this stuff out of the way."

"Hold it a minute." Taking one of the four-foot bars, Marco climbed to the top of the pile, balancing precariously. He tapped the end of the bar against the remaining rock covering the dome. He did it several times in different spots. Then he climbed back down.

"I'd swear it doesn't sound solid," he said, "but I could be wrong."

Piece by piece, the broken rock was carried down the sloping tunnel and dumped against the rockfall that blocked the remainder of the passage. It took about forty-five minutes to clear the area. Then they returned to the last cave, and Marco and Roberto went back up.

When Marco again emerged from the passageway, they waited for the blast.

It was less noisy than the previous one.

"I set a lighter charge," Marco explained as they made their way back up the tunnel. Once more there was a pile of broken rock in the middle of the chamber, and they entered in time to see the last of the dust and smoke being sucked up through a gaping hole in the roof.

Cosimo nodded his head in approval, and Marco grinned with pleasure.

"One more set," the American said, "and it should be large enough for a man to get through."

"I think that will not be necessary," Cosimo boomed, picking up one of the iron bars. "You may know much about explosives, boy, but I know the rocks of my mountains."

Standing astride part of the rubble, Cosimo gave a gigantic upward thrust with the bar against a huge shard of rock projecting over the hole. Dust filtered down. Again he struck. There was a sharp crack, and the piece of rock fell at Cosimo's feet.

Kimball and two of the biggest of the other partisans took the other bars and joined Cosimo, chipping away at the opening. In less than half an hour, they had made a hole large enough for even the big Cosimo.

Ed aimed his electric torch up through the hole, but the beam merely bounced off the thick clouds of dust now in the upper area. There was no real indication of what lay above.

"So, now it is my job once again," Joelle announced, hitching up her baggy trousers and taking the torch from Kimball's hand. She walked over to Cosimo. "Lift me up into the hole," she said simply.

Cosimo smiled and bowed, then lifted her like a feather. Those below saw her scramble over the lip of the hole and vanish. When she had been gone a full ten minutes, Kimball began to worry. He removed his miners' lamp and reached up and set it, still burning, on the upper edge of the hole, its light shining into the gaping void above.

When twenty minutes had elapsed, Kimball said: "That's long enough, I'm going up there and look for her."

At that instant, the dust-stained smiling face of Madame Gaussin peeked over the edge of the hole.

"Did you think I had gone for an aperitif, *Capitaine?*" she giggled. She swung her feet down through the hole, and Cosimo lifted her back to the floor.

"We are truly there, my friends," she announced happily, "although I am afraid that I may have miscalculated just a bit.

"Above us is a big limestone formation, full, like I say, with holes like cheese, only much bigger. One can climb from one to another like a monkey. About a hundred yards down, and up against the top of this limestone, are square blocks that have been made by man and put there by man. They are part of the castle, but I fear that we have found an escape tunnel and not the vault as I had hoped."

Kimball was elated. "That's not important, Joelle. If we can get into the tunnel, then we'll find a way into the vault. Let's go."

One by one, Cosimo lifted each man until he could pull himself up through the hole. The pry bars and axes were passed up, and then the big man levered himself up and into the limestone formation. Rather than leaving a light burning and waste batteries or carbide, Joelle secured the end of a ball of white yarn she had stuffed away and trailed it out behind her. Leading the way, she climbed up and to her left, the others trailing after. Ahead, in the dim beam of her headlamp, Ed could see what appeared to be a shelf of rock projecting out several feet from a sheer low wall. Like a gymnast, the agile Frenchwoman bellied herself over the edge of the shelf and sat down, her lamp beam pointing at an ancient brick.

"*Voilà*," she said proudly.

This time it was the mighty Cosimo who did the yeoman's work. Kimball and two others with bars worked alongside him. As each big hand-hewn stone was loosened, it was carefully handed back down the line to two of the partisans standing on another wide shelf several feet below. The blocks were stacked there.

The first layer of stone was peeled away to reveal a second wall. Cosimo attacked it immediately.

"Slowly, my friend," Kimball cautioned him. "We don't want to have the whole thing fall in on us."

There was a third layer yet to go.

An hour later, Cosimo's straining and bent pry bar carefully loosened a stone. With Kimball at the other end, they eased it backwards out of its place.

A small black, dank and musty hole showed where the block had been. Kimball reached through the hole and felt the underside of the wall. It was damp and mossy to the touch, and as he moved his arm about, he could feel the wall curving inward above them.

"Now we widen this," he said, "but only take out the lower blocks. I don't want to disturb that arch. One wrong block and we start all over."

One by one, the partisans slipped through the hole in the escape tunnel wall and followed the Proserpine team westward towards the main building of Vulcano Castle. The tunnel smelled fetid and unused. Moss was thick on the walls, and the air was heavy and humid the farther they moved from the hole into the limestone matrix.

Twice they eased themselves around jumbled piles of fallen masonry where sections of the ancient roof had given way. Another quarter of a mile brought them to a great heap of fallen stones blocking their way. But protruding from beneath the masonry was the long narrow stone of a step.

Ed threw his electric beam up along the fallen masonry. Water dripped from the hole in the ceiling where the blocks had once been. Roots of trees dangled like tentacles through the gaping hole. But at the top of the pile was the upper arch of a doorway, and beneath the arch the light played on what appeared to be the upper part of a massive door. They had found the vault.

The nine men, with Joelle doing what she could, worked to clear a path through the fallen stone and up the steps. Now they lifted each block carefully and set it aside, against the slight possibility that the vault might be occupied and sounds of their work be heard. It was back-breaking labor, teetering in near total darkness on loose heaps of stone and straining to lift and carry. It was another three hours before they had cleared a three-foot-wide path up the sixteen steps that led to the door and had removed all of the loose stone from the front of the door.

It was indeed an escape tunnel and had been used God only knew how many centuries ago. It had been designed to serve a dual purpose—to provide a means for the castle occupants to flee an invader and to slow up pursuit if followed.

Three great oaken bars lay across the outside of the door, resting in huge but rusting channels, where they had been dropped by the fleeing castle dwellers to bar pursuit.

Kimball tried to lift one but failed to budge it.

"Let me," Cosimo said, putting his shoulder under the upper bar and straining. The great wooden arm groaned and scraped and moved slightly, but the noise sounded like thunder to the silent people in the tunnel.

Kimball laid a cautionary hand on Cosimo's arm and then put his ear to the door. He could hear nothing, but it might only mean that the door was too thick for voices to penetrate.

He considered the problem for several minutes. Finally, he shrugged fatalistically. It was the only way into the castle. He moved up to Cosimo's side and put his own shoulder beside that of the huge man. Creaking and shrieking against the rusted supports, the bar came out of its channel. Other hands took it and carried it down the steps. The two men attacked the second barrier. It took their strength and those of two others before it finally came free.

Oddly, the third and lowest bar lifted out as though it had been put there only the day before.

Built centuries ago, long before the introduction of fixtures that recessed into the surrounding frame, there was nothing to keep the door from opening. Kimball uttered a silent prayer that no one had bricked over the old door from the inside. He indicated the handle with a thrust of his chin and nodded at Cosimo.

But, strong as Cosimo was, it would not open. The great iron hinges at the opposite side had rusted tight over the years.

By this time, there was no longer a need for cautious silence. If the room was occupied, then they had been heard, and there would be an armed reception committee waiting for them.

Against that possibility, Kimball sent all but himself, Cosimo and two of the biggest partisans back down the tunnel to wait by the hole. If they heard shots or commotion, they were to flee immediately.

Manning the four thick pry bars, the sweating men jammed them into the edge of the huge door and tugged.

The ancient tunnel echoed with the screech of rusted iron as the old hinges chipped, bent and gave way, and one broke from its moorings.

But the door was open, and through the slight crack they had made there was only darkness. All four let out their breaths collectively, then, with their bare hands, seized the edge of the opened door and pulled it wide enough for even Cosimo to squeeze through.

They were in an ancient storage vault beneath the castle, actually part of the main structure.

The beam of Kimball's lamp picked out broken barrels and old wooden crates. It was dry and musty in the chamber, and there were cobwebs throughout. At the far end of the big room, another stone stairway led up to a less massive door.

Carefully, Kimball picked his way across the room and up the far steps. This door opened inward, and though he pushed gently, it gave just an inch and stopped. Over the years, it had shrunk, and there was a half-inch gap between door and frame. Kimball placed an eye against the crack but saw only darkness beyond. He heard nothing, but he seemed to detect the slight odor of onions or garlic.

Satisfied the far room was empty, he played his torch up and down the crack. Apparently the door was held shut by a small wooden latch or bar. He reached back for his sheath knife and slid it through the crack under the latch. When he pushed up, the latch came easily, and he almost fell into the other room. Although the door creaked in protest, it was far less noisy than the lower vault door.

He was in another large storage room, one obviously in use. His beam played over crates of vegetables and cartons of canned goods stenciled with German markings. To his right and again up three short steps was another door, and from beneath it was bright light.

The way into the castle was now assured. He took one more quick look around the storage room and then went back to the door to the vault.

He closed it behind him, the wooden latch held up by his knife blade. When the door was closed, he lowered the knife and withdrew it. When pushed lightly, the door hit against the reseated latch. He rejoined Cosimo and the other two.

"Let's get out of here," he told the big man. "It's all clear and waiting for us up above."

In the beam of Kimball's light, they made their way back to the tunnel door and squeezed through. Marco, Joelle and the other Italians were waiting at the foot of the path cleared down the steps.

"We leave now," Kimball announced, "back to the main entrance."

The remaining packs of nitrostarch, along with the detonators and fuse, were left in the small cave where Ed, Marco and Joelle had spent the night. Joelle led them sure-footedly at a fast pace through the maze of tunnels back to the front cavern, where Adriana waited with her escort.

It was time for the next act of their scenario.

The weather that had stopped the Allied forces short of the Po River and bogged them down for the winter was now the weather that the Proserpine team needed for the final assault on Vulcano Castle. But by the time the group returned to the entrance to the caves, the rain had stopped.

After sentries were posted, the others gathered for an evening meal. It had already been turning dark as they emerged from the final passage into the large cavern. When he finished eating, Cosimo glanced over at the young American who was his son. Marco was smoking and talking with Adriana.

Cosimo stood up and beckoned to the younger man.

Marco frowned, then ground out his cigarette and followed Cosimo out of the cave and into the nearby trees. Cosimo walked fifty yards from the entrance and waited for Marco to reach him.

"What do you want, old man?" Marco asked belligerently.

"It is time to talk," Cosimo said quietly.

"I have nothing to say to you."

"Then listen," the partisan said. "There is nothing I can say or do that will ever wipe out the guilt from my soul. I have lived with it all these years, and now you come to bury me in it. So be it.

"But even as flowers will grow in a dung heap, there is some beauty to be found in the worst of all possible conditions. I speak of Adriana. I have seen you talking. Your sister is young and fragile, and yet much like you. She deserves better than you got. Christ on His cross knows that she deserves better than what I have given her or can give her in the future.

"This filthy war seems to go on forever, but I feel that it is coming to an end for me. If Adriana stays here, she faces only death or even worse, to end up in a German whorehouse. I have made a bargain with your Captain Eduardo. I agreed to help on this job, even though I think it may be the death of all of us, only because he agreed to take Adriana with him if you manage to get out of the castle alive. If you fail, I will be there and will be dead, too. I will try to have some of my people get her out of the region, but it will be a small chance.

"Eduardo's plans are good, and I think there is a chance that if we do not all die in the castle, you will get over the frontier."

He stopped and looked steadily at his son, their faces only inches apart.

"I have believed over the years that I gave you nothing," Cosimo continued, "but I was wrong. I gave you nothing you could eat or wear; I didn't even give you love. But I know and see now that I did give you something. I gave you my manhood, and you wear it well and honorably. You are a man.

"Adriana trusts you. Take care of her, Vincente, take care of her as the father of the two of you never did. She is worth all of the suffering I have ever had and face in hell forever. And so are you. I ask your word."

Marco turned and walked away a few paces, his back to Cosimo.

Then he retraced his steps.

"I have hated you for so many years," he said slowly. "I wanted to kill you. All I dreamed of was to find you someday and kill you."

"I know," his father said sadly, "it was spilling out of your eyes up there in the hills."

"But when the time came," Marco said, "I couldn't do it. And then there was Adriana. You are right. She does deserve more than you can give her. You have my word."

Cosimo wanted to step forward and embrace his son, but he knew that would not be permitted. With tears in his eyes, he bowed his great head in the dark.

"Thank you, my son."

They turned and walked back towards the entrance to

the cave. Suddenly Marco stopped and looked up at the big partisan.

"I don't know if I have inherited it from you," Marco said, "but I have watched you, these last few days. I no longer hate you, though I will never like you. But I can say with truth that you are indeed a man."

The American walked rapidly into the cave.

Cosimo entered a few minutes later, a small smile on his lips. He looked across, caught Kimball's eye and pointed to his watch. The Canadian nodded and rose.

"It is time."

Silently, with Cosimo in the lead, they worked their way through the trees and up the hill. In the dark, Cosimo laid a warning hand on Kimball's arm and pointed to his left. A few feet away was a deep gorge running through the mountain. On its floor, rail tracks shone faintly in the pale night light.

The two men moved quietly along the edge of the gorge until Cosimo dropped to one knee, waving Kimball down. They crept forward and peered over the edge. Along a lighted platform, thirty feet below, a pair of Wehrmacht soldiers in long greatcoats and steel helmets, rifles slung from their shoulders, paced the length of the platform.

A paved road and loading area led from the dock to the rear of the castle. A steel rail barrier and bumper guard marked the end of the line and the end of the siding that led up from the main yards in Aosta.

Cosimo and Kimball inched up on their bellies until they could peer over the edge of the gorge and keep the two sentries in sight. They squirmed in the dark and made themselves comfortable for a long wait.

It was precisely eight o'clock when a German Army weapons carrier drove up and stopped at the siding. From the back of the vehicle, two more soldiers climbed down, while a sergeant descended from the cab. Both sentries on duty came to attention in front of the sergeant as he eyed them up and down. Then, with a motion of his head, they relaxed and climbed into the back of the weapons carrier.

The vehicle drove off, leaving the relief men to take up their slow parade up and down the platform. The changing of the guard had taken less than two minutes from the time the weapons carrier appeared until it vanished down the road.

Throughout the long wait, Kimball and Cosimo took turns easing back from the edge of the gorge and into the trees to walk about for a few minutes and stretch aching legs.

At one minute before two in the morning, the lights of the weapons carrier flashed around the bend and pulled up at the siding. The earlier performance was repeated. When the vehicle vanished into the night, Cosimo and the Canadian backed away from the edge and made their way back through the forest to the cave. The night sentries at the rail siding stood six-hour tours of duty, changing at eight and at two.

Now all that remained was to pray for rain.

The sun was out most of the following day, with high clouds beginning to form along the upper reaches of the mountains by nightfall.

It was a welcome day of rest. Between naps and meals, Kimball and Cosimo drilled the group on the coming operation. At evening the rains came, continuing throughout the night and increasing in intensity the following morning. By four in the afternoon, fog had set in, and the rain was coming in torrents.

Kimball walked over to where Marco was sitting with Adriana. "Ready, Sergeant?"

Marco jumped to his feet. He leaned down to the girl. "There's nothing more to worry about," he assured her.

"Just do as we told you. By this time tomorrow, we'll be home free."

She reached up and pulled him down. "Please be careful, Vincente. I just found a brother. I don't want to lose him again." She placed a tender kiss on his cheek.

Blushing furiously, Marco followed Kimball into a side chamber. The Canadian was already stripping off his fatigues. The German Army officer uniforms were lying on the floor of the cave.

Moments later, Hauptmann Mannerheim and Waffen SS Lieutenant Shiller walked out of the cave in company of the most wanted Italian partisan in northern Italy.

The trio raced through the rain down the hillside to where a dirt track cut through the forest. Waiting there was a German Army staff car, stolen earlier in the afternoon under cover of the driving rain by one of Cosimo's accomplished partisans.

Kimball took the wheel, with Marco beside him and Cosimo in the back. It was already becoming dark from the storm, and Kimball carefully picked a way down the narrow muddy track for two miles until they emerged on the main east-west road leading from Aosta.

The staff car turned towards the town.

Nothing was moving in the rail yards when the car pulled up at the dispatcher's office. A gleam of light showed through a crack in the blackout curtains. Leaving Cosimo in the car, Kimball and Marco dashed to the door of the office and flung it open. The lone Italian rail employee sitting behind a battered desk with his feet up, reading a paper, nearly fell to the floor trying to get to his feet and out of the chair.

"You are the rail dispatcher in charge?" Kimball snarled at the frightened man.

"I do not speak German, Excellency," the man stammered.

Kimball switched to Italian and hoped that he wouldn't sound too fluent. He repeated his question.

"Yes, Excellency, I am."

Kimball reached into an inner pocket and pulled out papers that had been prepared at S.O.E. headquarters in Bari and which bore an almost perfect forgery of General Wilhelm Meirhausser's signature.

"Good. I am Captain Mannerheim, this is Lieutenant Shiller. We are of General Meirhausser's staff." He laid the papers on the desk in front of the Italian. "The general has ordered us to obtain a locomotive and a single goods car to be brought up to the headquarters siding immediately. There is an urgent shipment that must go out tonight."

"But, Captain," the dispatcher pleaded. "This weather. The tracks are washed out below Biella. Nothing is moving."

Kimball walked over to the desk and slammed his gloved hand down. "I'll tell you one thing that had better be moving, idiot," he said icily. "What had better be moving within the next few minutes is that locomotive and car to the Alpengruppe siding."

The Italian rolled his eyes. "There are no engineers on duty."

"Then get one."

"They have been given the time off until the tracks are repaired. I don't think any of them will come out on a night like this."

Kimball walked around the desk and slapped the man lightly across the face. "That is the last time you will say no to me. Understood? Now give me the name of an engineer. Come on, man, give me a name. Or would you rather give it to the Gestapo?"

The man was thoroughly frightened and visibly shaking. Outside, the cold heavy rain beat against the tin shack.

"There is Luigi Delvecchio," he stuttered. "Perhaps he might go."

"Where does he live?"

"Beside the postal office, Excellency," the Italian replied. "But he will need a fireman."

"That won't be necessary," Kimball said. "We have brought one of our own workers for that. He is familiar with the job. Now, you go fetch this Luigi whatever his name is, but first, show us the locomotive that will be used and I will have my man fire it up."

"Number Six came in a half hour ago from the north, and I think there is still fire in the box, Excellency. It sits right out there." He pointed through the foggy window.

"Has it been turned?"

"No, Excellency."

"Better still," Kimball said. "For that short a trip we will back it up the siding to headquarters. Now, get your coat and we will get your engineer. Lieutenant Shiller will go with you to make sure you find the place. I will be kind to you, peasant. Lieutenant Shiller will even take you there in my car and bring you back. Now get out of here."

Seconds later, Cosimo came into the shack; Marco was driving the terrified dispatcher into the town.

Kimball pointed out the locomotive they would be using. "You know anything about those things, Cosimo?"

"Eduardo, Eduardo, will you never learn? Cosimo knows something about everything. We have been stealing these things for four years now. Of course, I know. I can run it as well as that engineer."

"Good, get out there and make sure it has a full head of steam and is ready to roll. And see if you can locate an empty car we can pick up without too much backing and switching. We'll back out, car first, up the siding."

Cosimo ran through the rain to the steam locomotive.

Kimball paced impatiently in the small heated shack. He kept looking at his watch. At this point, timing was critical. They had to have the engine and its car at the siding just minutes after the new sentries came on duty at eight o'clock. It was now past six.

Marco was back in fifteen minutes with the dispatcher and an angry, scowling engineer.

"What's this terrible hurry?" the engineer demanded of Kimball. "Nobody's going anywhere tonight, not until the tracks are repaired. Which way do you plan to take the train from the siding? You can't go south."

Marco's fist suddenly shot out and smashed into the man's midriff. The engineer gagged and doubled over.

"You do not use that tone of voice to a German officer, pig," Marco yelled, "and you do not ask questions that are none of your business. Now get your useless ass out there and into that locomotive. Do you understand me?"

The engineer clutched his stomach and nodded. Marco shoved him to the door and followed him out into the rain.

Kimball pointed to the papers on the desk. "These are your orders, to keep your record straight," he said to the dispatcher. "You will see Herr General Meirhausser's signature at the bottom, all in order."

"Thank you, Captain," the dispatcher said humbly.

Kimball turned to go. "And the next time you get orders from the German Army, let us hope that you will move faster, yes?"

He walked out of the office and ran for the staff car. In the yards, the locomotive with Cosimo and Marco and the engineer was moving down the tracks, approaching a freight car. Kimball smiled and put the staff car in gear. He drove to the edge of the town and pulled into a grove of trees bordering the switch that would take the two-piece train up the siding. Moments later, it rumbled into view, moving slowly. Marco was hanging from the step and jumped lightly to the ground as the engine rolled past. As soon as he was off, the train picked up speed. The American ran to the staff car and jumped in.

"Any problems?" Ed asked as he put the car in gear.

"None," Marco replied. "Cosimo was waiting for us. As soon as the engineer got aboard, that big *paisano* put a gun at his head. He'll cooperate."

Kimball drove into the pouring rain back towards the forest road.

Although they had been on the platform only minutes since the changing of the guard, both German sentries were sodden and sullen, cursing the fact that they had nearly six more hours of it before they were relieved.

Suddenly the lights illuminating the platform went out.

"Must be the damned rain," one of the Germans called out. "Short circuit or something. I hope the damned phone is working." He groped through the dark for the post that held the field telephone connecting them to the castle. He never reached it.

Less than two minutes later, the train rumbled around a curve and backed slowly into the siding.

The lights were again burning, and two of Cosimo's men were waiting for the train, wearing the uniforms of the dead sentries. The train came to a halt, and out of the dark three more of the partisans appeared, together with Adriana and Joelle. Two of them helped the women climb into the empty freight car and then climbed in after them. The third ran to the cab of the locomotive and leaped aboard.

The sullen Italian engineer sat silently on his seat, glaring at Cosimo.

"Stay here with this one," Cosimo directed his man. "Make sure he keeps his fire going and the pressure up. It must be right here on the dial at all times." He showed the partisan where the needle should be. "If he tries anything, kill him."

The partisan nodded, and Cosimo swung down from the cab. He signaled to the two German-uniformed partisans to follow him and ran for the road that took him around the lip of the gorge and back into the forest. The two followed as he sped for the cave.

The others were waiting for them when they burst wetly out of the night. Kimball and Marco still wore German officers' uniforms, but Marco and four of the partisans also carried gas masks slung at one side and small knapsacks of gas grenades on the other. All were armed with their beloved Thompson machine guns.

Kimball checked their equipment and ran a quick review of the groupings. He had little doubt that Riva would be waiting for them in her room. The big question still remaining, and one that only she could answer, was the location of the plans. Bancroft and he had both agreed that they would be locked in a safe, one which Meirhausser alone had access to. But where within the multiroomed castle that safe might be was something only Riva could tell them.

Once inside the castle, the first route would be to her room. Then seven men of the team, led by Marco and Cosimo, would take up defensive positions against German discovery and attack. The other two men would stay close to Kimball as protection for Riva, while Kimball, with his extensive training and field experience, attempted to open the safe and extract the papers. Once they were secured, everyone would execute the most familiar of military exercises—getting the hell out of there.

If anything should happen to Kimball while he was working on the safe, Marco was to take over and finish blowing it.

"Any questions?"

There was silence as men tugged equipment into place and checked arms.

"Good, let's go." Kimball turned and moved into the convoluted passageway leading to the castle. During the long waiting the day before, Joelle and one of the men had traversed the entire length of the cave system and up through the limestone to the point where they had broken through the escape-tunnel wall. Now, Joelle's strand of white yarn was strung the entire distance from the front cavern.

"You will be coming out of there, probably in a very great rush," she told Kimball after his flat refusal to allow her to accompany the assault group as guide, "and you may have lost your lights. The yarn will take you out in the dark, though slowly."

The now familiar route was covered much faster. They reached the last cave, where the extra explosives had been stored, in less than an hour.

Marco had also been into the cave during the preceding day. Ten pounds of charges, together with detonators and extra fuses, were stowed in a backpack. Forty pounds of the remaining nitrostarch were stacked and taped into a loose pile beside the entrance to the passageway into the small domed cave. A detonator, with fuse, was already in place. The backpack with the remaining charges Marco hauled back to the main entrance, where he propped it by the outer exit, to be seized on the run, if necessary, as they escaped. Another thirty pounds were in packs to be carried by the others.

Trying to move fast and occasionally banging into the tunnel walls, Kimball winced at the thought of the two ounces of pure liquid nitroglycerine wrapped in a thick wad of cotton batting and taped under his left armpit.

His imagination magnified the sound of the muffled snorts and occasional clicks of equipment as the others crept and crawled behind him. When they reached the end of the passageway with the hole above leading to the escape tunnel, he checked his watch. They had moved into the tunnel shortly after nine. It was now a quarter to eleven at night— less than three hours to complete the job and get back to the waiting train.

Another ten minutes and they were slipping past the partially opened oak door into the first vault. They crossed the room to the door to the second storage area. Again, Kimball started to use his knife to lift the wooden latch.

Cosimo tapped him on the arm. "Let me and a couple of my people go in front, Eduardo," he whispered. "We have much experience in handling this kind of a job. We can take out sentries who will be dead and silent before they know they are dying."

"Get them up here," Kimball said, "and the three of you stay right behind me. But I have to lead. I know this place, and I know where we're going. If we spot guards, then you can go to work."

Cosimo hissed a command, and two of the partisans moved to his side. Ed's knife lifted the latch, and the commando group moved silently across the storage room to the far door.

Now, only a dim light showed through the space beneath the other door.

Kimball put his shoulder to the door, and slowly and carefully pressed down on the more modern and conventional door catch. Behind him, Cosimo and his two companions held their Thompsons aimed at the door, while the others back in the dark kept their weapons at ready.

The handle turned easily in Kimball's grip, and the door inched open. He paused and listened. There was only silence from the other room. Slowly and gently he let his weight ease the door open, holding the handle to prevent its sudden swing. Inch by inch, the door opened into the main kitchen of the castle. It was deserted at this hour, with only a dim incandescent light bulb dangling from a twisted wire over the huge sink as a night light.

Quick mental images of both the blueprints of the castle and his own knowledge of the place kaleidoscoped through Ed's head as the Proserpine team padded across the deserted room, the heavy aroma of cabbage and cooking oil hanging in the air. A narrow door at the right rear of the kitchen opened onto a flight of narrow corkscrewing stone steps leading up to the main level of the castle. They climbed quickly and silently, each man looking around as he crossed the kitchen to the stairway for landmarks he might need if left on his own to escape.

Riva's room, if she had not changed it, was on the far side of the castle, immediately adjacent to the northwest wall tower. It was too risky to try to work their way up and through the occupied portions of the building to reach her. The stairway from the kitchen, really a back passage for quick access rather than the main entrance, ended in a small open arch at the end of a long dimly lighted corridor. Near the head of the staircase, Kimball went to his stomach and carefully lifted his head, covered with the black tight-fitting seaman's wool cap, over the lip of the top step. The corridor was empty. In the distance, he could hear the sound of voices and the faint laughter of a man. It would be coming from the central hall at the entrance to the castle. He rose and went a few paces into the corridor, then slowly opened another small door leading to the inner courtyard. Sheets of rain, coming down so hard that the pounding could be heard even through the thick walls of the old building, hit his face. He ignored the weather and slipped quickly into the dark wet courtyard, his back pressed against the castle wall, hidden in the black shadows of the building. Cosimo and the others were at his shoulder.

Two large shielded lights on their right shone wetly through the rain, marking the main doors into the castle; on both sides of the courtyard at the outer corners other lights were burning. But the torrential and bitterly cold rain effectively diffused the light, and most of the courtyard was in deep darkness. The Proserpine group had to cross the courtyard to get to the far wall tower.

Still with back to wall, Kimball sidestepped towards the near corner to the main building, eyes probing the dark for the sentries he knew must be there.

Cosimo touched his shoulder, and Kimball stopped. The big partisan had seen something. Gripping the Canadian's shoulder in a signal to wait, Cosimo eased his great bulk past Kimball and vanished into the darkness along the wall. Moments later, he loomed again out of the rain and indicated that Kimball could proceed. Moving faster now, but still in the shadows of the wall and now soaking with rain, they reached the corner. Kimball stumbled and looked down at the dead body of the German sentry. Silently, Cosimo and two of the others hoisted the body and then heaved it upwards; it fell with a dull thud atop the wide parapet wall that separated the inner and outer courtyards. Closing on the open gate in the wall that led to the main entrance, Kimball never saw the flashing dark shadow of a man racing across the courtyard, caught momentarily in the dim light filtering through the open gate.

Kimball peeked around the edge of the wall; the main doors to the castle were closed against the rain, although light came from partially shuttered windows at either side of the doors. He motioned for the attack party to go to the ground. He put his lips to Cosimo's ear and whispered a command. The partisan nodded and turned to pass the instructions down the line.

The Canadian peered once more around the corner and then scuttled quickly on all fours across the lighted gate and into the deep shadows on the far side. One by one, the others followed. When it appeared that all had crossed, Kimball rose and again moved, back to the wall towards the far corner of the courtyard and the entrance to the wall tower. He squinted, brushing the rain from his face and eyes as he tried to locate the other sentry who had to be patrolling the far side of the yard.

Over the pounding of the rain, Kimball suddenly clutched at his submachine gun, whirling as the whispered voice came out of the darkness ahead.

"Proserpine."

Virtually invisible in his black Waffen SS uniform, Marco slid up to him, grinning broadly. He winked and signaled for Kimball and the others to follow. At the far corner of the wall the other sentry lay dead, his gaping throat already washed clean of most of the blood by the pouring rain.

Kimball cut off an angry comment, then patted Marco on the shoulder. The American had spotted the guard from the opposite side of the courtyard and, without waiting, had made his own command decision.

The door to the wall tower opened easily, and the attackers moved out of the rain onto the dark stone steps curving up the tower to the battlements at top. Only faint light filtered through the three slotted archers' windows at the sides of the round tower.

There was a landing at the upper floor of the castle, and then the steps continued on to the open battlements. Time was down to less than three hours.

Kimball eased open the door and peered down the long corridor running the width of the building. To the left were doors leading to the sleeping rooms of the castle lords. At the right, another stone wall was broken by waist-high open arches that looked down on the main hall of the building. A massive stone stairway rose majestically from the hall below to the center of the balcony corridor. Tapestries and paintings adorned the left wall between the doors, and dim ornamental electric fixtures projected from the inner wall, fixtures that originally had held rush torches and candles. Odd pieces of furniture, tables and period-piece chairs, were scattered down the long passage.

The corridor itself was empty. Now the sounds of the

Germans on night duty in the central hall came clearly to Kimball as he looked and listened. The conversation was quiet, and there was no indication that the courtyard sentries had yet been missed. He turned and signaled Cosimo and the others to wait, then pointed to the first door on the left wall. The big partisan nodded.

Kimball slipped carefully through the doorway into the long hall, staying well against the inner wall and crouching slightly to avoid being seen from the main hall below. He tried the handle to Riva's door. It was locked. Gently, he knocked. There was no response. Again he knocked. Faintly, through the heavy door, he heard her voice.

"Who is it?"

Rather than risk raising his voice, he again knocked softly. Seconds passed, and this time her voice was closer. She repeated the challenge.

"Eduardo," he called softly, glancing anxiously over his shoulder.

Instantly, the door burst open, and Riva hurled herself at Kimball, arms about his neck, face buried in his chest. Half-carrying her, Kimball moved into the room and closed the door.

"Eduardo, oh my Eduardo. You don't know how I've waited for this moment, knowing you were coming and so frightened." Riva was crying openly, still clutching him to her slim negligéed body.

All the bitterness and jealousy he had nurtured during the past two years vanished in her embrace. Gently, he raised her tear-stained face and smiled. He leaned down, and they kissed longingly and lengthily. Then he pulled away. "Later, *carissima*," he said. "Now get dressed and quickly. I have men in the tower, and I want to get them in here. Plan for a rough trip. You're going out with us, after you show me where the plans are."

She smiled with dazzling happiness and moved quickly

to her adjacent dressing room. "They are in Meirhausser's private study, down the far corridor, darling. I shall be but a moment."

Kimball smiled happily to himself and slipped out the door to the entrance to the wall tower. Ten seconds later, the Proserpine assault team was inside Riva's room with the door again closed. The dripping commandos stood awkwardly and uncomfortably in the scented feminine surroundings, trying to minimize the water running from their soaked clothing and pooling on the rich carpeting. The two partisans still wearing the pot helmets and Wehrmacht greatcoats they had taken from the train sentries literally poured water to the floor.

When Riva reappeared, she was dressed in wool slacks, hiking boots, warm blouse and woolen sweater. She carried a down jacket over her arm, its pockets bulging with small personal items snatched from her dressing room and bath cabinets.

"I am Riva di Savoldi," she announced to the admiring but tongue-tied group.

"There is no time for introductions to all," Ed said. "This is American Sergeant Vincent Marco, and this monster is Cosimo. The rest you will meet later."

Riva surveyed Vinnie's wet but well-fitting Waffen SS uniform. "It fits you well, Sergeant," she said half-seriously, "but it is not at all becoming to you."

"Riva, please, the plans. Where are they?"

Quickly, she outlined the current status of the castle. "You have been the object of a massive search, Eduardo, ever since they found your parachutes and that Fascist Lucca came here to tell the Gestapo he had seen you."

Cosimo's eyes widened momentarily at that last bit of information, and he glanced knowingly at his men, his hand slashing across his neck.

"Even tonight, they now suspect that you are close by.

A staff car was found missing from the motor pool late this evening, and the Gestapo man, that pig Koppfman, is certain it was you who took it. They have their troops out all over the town and around the castle. Both Koppfman and Willi" —she stammered briefly—"that is, General Meirhausser, are down below in what they call their field quarters where they can be reached instantly if you are discovered. That is a small bit of luck.

"But, Eduardo, there are two armed guards outside his private study, and his safe, with the plans, is in that room. How will you ever get past them without raising an alarm? There are several dozen German soldiers now in the castle and literally several hundred more in the immediate vicinity. I still don't know how you got here."

"You'll find out when we leave," Kimball said. "You say there are just two men on guard by the study door?"

She bobbed her head.

"Wehrmacht or Waffen?"

"Wehrmacht. Regular German Army men."

Kimball pulled the drawings of the castle from an inner pocket, spread them on Riva's bed and called his people together around him.

"Point out which room is the study, Riva."

She indicated a room adjacent to the far wall tower, almost directly above the castle kitchen. The main structure was laid out in an L-shape, with her own bedroom at the upper end of the L and the study near the tip of the foot. The long corridor outside her door was the upright length of the L.

"Once I'm in that room, Marco," Kimball said, "you and Cosimo set up a defense along the corridor. When we leave, we go down this stairway back to the kitchen. It's an extension of the one we came up to the courtyard, so we'll be going out just as we came in, once we hit the main landing. Try and jam or barricade both the main kitchen door and the door at the top of the small stairs that we went through to get out into the courtyard. It might slow them up.

"Cosimo, you and Marco know what to do about those sentries, right?"

The partisan bowed his head.

"Riva, you stay with me in the study. Two of these men will be with us and will see that you are safe and get out, if anything should happen to me."

"Oh, Eduardo, don't even say such a thing."

"We'll pull it off, little one. All right, let's move."

This time, Cosimo led the way out of the bedroom suite down the long corridor, keeping low and pressing against the inner wall out of sight of the men below. His two partisans and Kimball in their German uniforms were behind him, the others trailing along closely.

At the foot of the corridor, Cosimo crawled on his belly across the hall and cautiously eased his head around the corner. A pair of sentries was standing casually at either side of the far door, talking softly in violation of regulations. Cosimo pulled back and nodded.

Kimball and the two uniformed partisans rose, still against the far wall. The Canadian's wool cap had been stuffed into a side pocket and all of them were still wet to the skin but unaware of discomfort. Kimball tugged at the skirt of his jacket and threw back his shoulders. With the two uniformed partisans following him, he walked militarily down the corridor towards the study door. As he approached, both sentries spotted the officer's uniform and clicked to rigid attention, chins tucked deeply, heads back, eyes locked on a spot over Kimball's head as he stopped directly in front of them.

They were still looking over his head as the hidden long knives in the partisans' hands sliced in and upwards in enemy midriffs, ripping both lungs and heart. One sentry opened his mouth to scream, but a hand was clamped over it before he could make a sound. Softly, the partisans eased the bodies to the floor, catching the slung machine pistols before they could strike the stones.

Secure in his authority, Meirhausser never bothered to lock the study door. The bodies of the dead sentries were dragged into the room and their places taken by the two partisans. Cosimo, who had been watching the entire operation, waved to the others. Immediately, the two assigned to watch over Riva rushed her down the corridor and into the room where Kimball was already studying the massive old safe that stood at one side of the study. One of the partisans was also carrying a knapsack which he now handed to Kimball.

The Canadian pulled out an electric drill and a half dozen diamond-tipped drills, together with a long extension cord. A pair of reading lamps flanked the top of Meirhausser's desk. Kimball followed the wiring and found an electrical outlet. Drill in hand, he went to work on the safe.

In the corridor, Cosimo whispered to Marco, "I will attend to the lower doors now and then return."

Even as they whispered, there was a sudden upsurge in the voices of the men on duty below. Neither Cosimo nor Marco were fluent enough in German to understand what was being said, but alarm was evident in the tones. They heard the sound of the big front doors of the hall banging open and the pounding of feet. The sentries had been found either missing or dead.

Secrecy was over, and Marco prepared his men for the fighting. He hissed a word to the two guarding the study door, and in an instant they happily shed the German helmets and topcoats and raced to a corner of the corridor that commanded its length. There was a growing uproar from the hall below but still no indication of anyone coming up the main stairs.

The four partisans and Marco scattered in a small group

in the shadows of furniture, away from the dim light at the corner of the L. Gas masks were hanging from their necks, and their Thompsons, each with a round in the chamber, pointed down the corridor at the top of the great staircase.

Crouched against the stones of the outer wall, Marco laid a half-dozen gas grenades on the floor in front of him, tapes pulled, ready to be thrown. Cosimo snaked down the length of the shorter corridor from the rear stairs and tapped Marco on the foot.

"The doors are blocked as well as I could manage," he whispered, "but they won't stop them for long. I will go down and cover you there when you pull out."

Marco winked, and his father slithered away towards the darkened opening of the stairs.

Inside the study, Kimball had drilled two of the five holes he needed and was pressing into the third. Each hole had blunted and made useless a bit, and he prayed that none would snap in the process. He had only five. Across the room, Riva watched with anxious eyes. The two Italians were pressed close to the wall at either side of the door, listening for the first sounds of alarm from the corridor.

Boot leather slapped against stone as the men in the hall heard what sounded like a lone person coming up the stairs from the hall below. At the top of the steps, a Wehrmacht captain paused in the corridor, then turned in the direction of the study. Marco waved for his men to remain hidden.

The German came striding down the corridor to the corner and bumped into a Waffen SS officer. Momentarily off guard and embarrassed, he stepped back and murmured an apology. The American's slashing hand caught him across the throat, crushing his larnyx and sending him to the floor.

Marco dragged the inert form around the corner and went back to wait.

Inside the study, Kimball was changing bits to start the fourth hole. The whine of the drill shrilled through the room.

It was a full five minutes before a shout came from the stairs as someone called out to the man Marco had killed. The German shouted again and then came running up the staircase when he got no answer from the officer or from either of the sentries posted at the study door.

Kimball cut through the fourth hole and prepared to drill his final cut.

The second Wehrmacht officer stopped at the top of the stairs and again called out, "Fritz, *wo ist?*"

In the two seconds of silence that followed, the man's face blanched, and he spun and raced back down the stairs, yelling commands.

In his darkened corner, Marco slipped on his gas mask and turned so that his companions could see him. Silently, they followed suit.

There was a series of shouted commands from the main hall below, and the invaders heard the pounding of hobnailed boots as German troopers came running into the echoing chamber. Suddenly a pair of powerful flashlight beams played across the walls and up and down the short corridor where the study was located. The lights passed well above the crouching partisans of Marco's team.

More crisp commands came from below, along with the sounds of bolts being pulled on weapons and then the clicking of hobnails on the main stairs, moving up quickly. Marco threw one quick look over his shoulder at the study door in the hope that Kimball was ready. The door remained closed; he turned back and picked up a gas grenade, holding the pull-pin in his left hand.

In the shadows, four Thompsons on full automatic fire aimed down the hall.

Ten German troopers, led by a sergeant and followed by an officer, all with weapons at the ready poured up the stairs and into the corridor. They paused momentarily at the landing, and Marco heaved the spluttering grenade down the hall. It popped, and a cloud of tear gas burst out as the four Thompsons opened fire. The noise was deafening in the echoing vaulted building.

Almost in the same motion, Marco leaned through the nearest arched opening in the outer wall of the corridor and sent another gas grenade arcing and spluttering through the air to hit the floor below, where it released another blanket of gas.

Six of the German soldiers died under the smashing barrage of the four Thompsons. Three of the soldiers and the officer at the rear had thrown themselves prone when the grenade was hurled. When the guns opened fire, they rolled and bounced back down the stairs, coughing and blinded.

The crashing, echoing roar of the partisan guns covered the muffled explosion from within the study as Kimball's carefully placed nitro charges blew. He had waved Riva and the partisans to the wall to either side of the safe as he lit the fuse, then he threw himself atop Riva to shield her from the blast.

Even as the smoke was starting to pour from the ruptured door, Kimball was on his feet, shouldering the hot metal aside. Quickly, he pulled papers from the smashed safe.

Riva was at his side. "It is called *Festung Bergskrieg,*" she said quickly. "It is also known as Project *Wachter.*"

She uttered the code name just as Kimball reached for a large green folder, tied and bound with tape and sealed with wax. On the face in Germanic script was, "Project *Wachter.*"

"Got it," Kimball exclaimed exultantly. "Let's get out of here."

Pushing Riva ahead of him, he stuffed the plans inside his tunic and grabbed his weapon from the floor. Fumes of gas were seeping under the door and making their eyes water.

"Tear gas," he warned Riva and the two partisans. "Hold your breath and close your eyes as much as possible.

Go out on the run and turn left. The door to the stairs is just four paces away. All right. Go," he yelled as another burst of fire came from the hall.

One of the partisans jerked the door open, and the four ran from the room.

Kimball paused in the gas-filled corridor. "Marco," he yelled. "Go, go, go."

Coughing and half-blinded, he groped for the stairwell and nearly fell as he plunged through the door.

Marco waved to the two partisans at his side and pointed to the door. Still in gas masks, they ran for the stairs. When they had disappeared from sight, he waved the second pair to the stairs.

Wearing gas masks, another German assault team came racing up the steps and directly into Marco's fire as he crouched against the outer wall, covering the partisans' escape. Blending with the deafening roar of his submachine gun was the even louder blast of a German hand grenade lobbed up from below into the corridor behind him. The blast knocked Marco flat, and when he rolled over and looked, both partisans lay dead at the end of the corridor, one of them sprawled facedown across the first steps of the stairway.

The American sergeant pressed against the cover of the outer wall and scuttled down the short corridor. Opposite the stairwell, he crawled across the floor and went headfirst over the body of the dead partisan, sliding and tumbling and finally stopping long enough to swing his legs around and get to his feet. Just below, another Thompson spewed its familiar automatic burst.

Cosimo was standing on the landing, wisps of smoke trickling from the barrel of the submachine gun. The door to the outer corridor was riddled.

At the sight of Marco, Cosimo burst into a huge grin and spun down the steps to the kitchen, his son almost riding his back. They raced for the storeroom. The door to the kitchen buckled and shattered as German troopers battered at the barricade of tables, chairs and a chest that Cosimo had piled there.

At the entrance to the storage room, Marco turned and tossed another gas grenade into the kitchen just as the far door gave way. He fled into the dark after Cosimo, who stood at the vault end of the room, holding an electric torch shielded in his hands to guide his son.

Marco snatched off the gas mask and drew a deep breath of the damp musty air.

"Go, old man, I'm right behind you. I lost my light."

Cosimo ran down the short steps into the vault as the American threw the last of his gas grenades into the storeroom and followed.

By the time they reached the floor of the tunnel, there was no sign of the rest of the party.

Father and son ran for the hole in the wall. As Marco slipped through to follow Cosimo's light down the limestone maze, he could hear sounds of pursuit behind them. Despite his size, Cosimo again evidenced the agility of a mountain goat as he whipped through the limestone, gathering up the guideline of yarn as he went. It was slowing him down.

"Forget it, old man," his son panted. "I can stop them another way. Move it, move it."

Cosimo dropped through the hole in the dome of the cave and waited momentarily until Marco was down and could follow his light. Then Cosimo turned and scrambled into the passageway leading to the main cavern. When they reached the first small storage chamber, Marco called a halt.

The pair hunkered down at the far side of the chamber beside the pile of explosives Marco had set earlier. It had taken father and son four minutes to traverse the passageway from the end to the chamber where they waited. But it would take the Germans longer, being unfamiliar with the tunnel and hampered by weapons and equipment. But they did have the yarn to follow.

Silently, father and son waited in the chamber, listening. Marco cut the fuse for seven minutes. From out of the darkness behind them, they heard the faint echo of voices.

"Now," Marco ordered and put a match to the end of the fuse. Cosimo was already moving down the narrow tunnel. The American grabbed the packsack with the remaining explosives and went squirming after the partisan. They were crossing the next big dome, where they had slept coming in, when the earth shook, and dust and small debris drifted down the stone walls.

Marco grinned at his father, and they raced into the last length of their journey out.

Behind them, more than a half mile of the cave system collapsed under the force of the explosion. The first two German troopers had emerged into the small chamber, the passageway behind them jammed with others, when the lead man saw the fuse sputtering in the dark across the chamber.

His first instinct was to rush over and stamp it out, but new fear and panic seized him. He screamed and tried to scramble past his comrade and back into the tunnel just as a third trooper crawled out. The nitrostarch exploded.

The first three Germans into the chamber, as well as those behind them in the tunnel and the entrance cave, died in the cave-in, along with three others still in the limestone honeycomb that also shattered in the blast.

Pursuit from behind was ended.

Kimball was waiting at the outer entrance to the cave when Marco and Cosimo emerged from the passageway. They ran to him.

He grabbed them both in a short embrace of happiness.

"Where are the others?" Cosimo asked.

"Already on their way to the train. I waited for you."

It was still pouring as the trio ran from the cavern into

the forest, Cosimo again in the lead. Over the beat of the rain, they could hear the sounds of distant motors; from the direction of the castle, a dull glow lighted the low clouds as floodlights bathed the main courtyard where truck after truck of German troopers was being loaded for the search. Stumbling after Cosimo's fast-moving figure, Kimball took time to look at his watch. He groaned inwardly and tried to move faster. It was already five minutes after two in the morning. Perhaps the excitement might have delayed the changing of the guard at the siding.

They came sliding and slipping up to the edge of the gorge and peered cautiously over the side. The engine still stood there, emitting small puffs of steam. Standing beside the steps to the cab was Roberto. A German weapons carrier was parked at the side of the platform, but there was no sign of the German sentries.

Kimball, Cosimo and Marco hurried down the far side of the gorge and ran for the train. Roberto swung around, gun ready to fire, and from the door of the freight car six other barrels were trained on them. Roberto let out a small yelp of relief as he recognized the huge figure of his leader.

"You took long enough," he said casually as they panted to a halt at his side.

"What happened over there?" Cosimo asked, pointing to the weapons carrier.

Roberto shrugged. "They met with an accident."

Kimball laughed and clapped him on the back. "All the others aboard?"

"G'vanni and Pietro haven't shown up."

"I'm sorry," Marco said. "They won't be coming."

Cosimo and Roberto stared at Marco for a second, and then both gave little sighs of sorrow.

Roberto crossed himself. "Receive them, O Christ," he muttered.

"Amen," Kimball said softly, then turned to the engine. "Time to roll this thing."

Cosimo climbed up after Kimball, and the other two ran for the open door of the already moving freight car.

Headlights doused, with only the faint glow of the fire-box seeping around the boiler door, the Proserpine Express rolled slowly down the slight incline into the dark storm of the night.

◆　　◆　　◆

The great doors to the castle were thrown wide in disregard of the driving rain and wind. The last lingering stink of cordite and tear gas was being sucked out of the great hall. General Wilhelm Meirhausser, still red-eyed but in full field uniform, stood beside Gestapo Major Conrad Koppfman, drawing concentric circles on a large-scale map of the terrain surrounding the castle and most of Aosta.

A muted scream came from deep in the corridor at the rear where the two German doctors were working on one of the more seriously wounded soldiers cut down by the Proserpine group fire.

Out of sight and deep below them, other men, including a pair of medics, all wearing gas masks, tried to probe the dense cloud of dust and tear gas still hanging in the still air of the escape tunnel and the ancient storage vault. The walls and ceiling of the centuries-old tunnel bulged and creaked ominously, weakened even further by the earthshaking effect of the explosive charge. Their electric-torch beams were diffused by the debris in the air, but they could see the hole in the tunnel wall a few feet ahead and could hear the moans of injured men, trapped in the limestone honeycomb but still alive.

The rescue team reached the exit hole and threw light beams into the cavity. The bloodied and dust-streaked face of a Wehrmacht trooper looked up at them beseechingly. The lower part of the man's body was hidden and pinned by fallen rock. The noncom in charge of the detail waved his men into the hole, and they began heaving loose rock from the trapped trooper. The sergeant and two others followed the sounds of more moans and low German voices eastward towards the spot where the underground chamber had been. Of the cave that Marco had blown through the roof, and Cosimo and the others had widened to give the team access up to the tunnel, not a trace remained. All had collapsed. Sole indication that there might have been something under the jumble of blasted rock was the body of another German soldier, eyes still open in death, one arm and his head emerging from the limestone that had crushed him from the chest down as he had scrambled towards the now nonexistent hole in the cave roof.

The staccato roar of Thompson submachine guns had brought Meirhausser and Koppfman out of their field cots at the rear of the main hall.

Both had seized handguns and run jacketless into the hall at the moment Marco's second gas grenade had come sailing from the overhead arch and burst on the stone floor. The two officers, blinded by the eye-searing gas, had turned and groped their way back into their offices to find gas masks. More gunfire had erupted from above.

Meirhausser slammed the door to his office, and, before donning his mask, dipped his face into the water-filled washbasin on the table beside his bed, clearing his vision enough to see blurrily through the lens of his mask. Again he rushed to the hall as other German troops came pouring in from both the front and side entrances.

The Wehrmacht officer who had been with the first assault team was now assembling a second, screaming orders to don gas masks.

The general edged his way around the great pillars flanking the hall on three sides until he had the short upper corridor in view. He watched as another assault team moved more cautiously up the main staircase and saw the flashes of the partisan guns from the corner of the L. Above, and in the far end of the corridor where it ended in the narrow stairwell leading to the kitchen and pantry, another gun barrel winked with orange and black-tipped fire.

There was no doubt in Meirhausser's mind as to the objective of the invasion. The bastards were trying to break into his private office and into his safe. He turned and waved to a noncom crouched a few feet away with a dozen other men behind him, waiting for an opportunity to rush the stairs. The general's voice roared through the muffling mask. The noncom nodded and ran to his men, waving them towards the rear wall, out of line of fire, and then raced under the overhang towards the first level floor entry to the far staircase.

A potato masher hand grenade sailed up from the main hall through one of the upper arches to burst with a deafening roar in the corridor above. It was at that instant that Kimball's nitro had exploded, blowing off the lock to Meirhausser's safe. The general never heard it.

Then it was over, almost as quickly as it had started. There was the hammering of another Thompson from the far corner of the main hall near the entry to the stairwell, then virtual silence. No sound came from the upper level. Koppfman, crouching beside the general, heard the muffled crashes and curses of the troopers who threw themselves at the barred door to the stairway. Again, nothing. The thick pall of gas and gun smoke was already thinning, pouring out under the eaves of the outer doors.

Meirhausser snatched off his mask and sniffed, then stood and waited for a full fifteen seconds. More than twenty Wehrmacht and Waffen troopers crouched beside the main stairs, peering up, guns on full load. The general ran across the floor, expecting gunfire to follow. When he reached the foot of the stairs without attack, he yelled at the lieutenant leading the group beside the staircase.

"Up," he screamed, "get up there and get those bastards."

In unison, they rose and pounded up the stairs, the lead

men throwing themselves flat as they hit the last step, then sending a stream of fire down the corridor to the corner where the attack had originated. When there was no return fire, the soldiers jumped to their feet and ran a zigzag pattern to the corner. The corridor was deserted, and the door to Meirhausser's office stood open. At the far end lay the bodies of the two partisans where they had fallen when the stick grenade had exploded.

Thirty seconds later, Meirhausser stood at the door to his office and screamed curses at the sight of the battered safe, its door askew and open, papers scattered on the floor. It took just a moment to determine that the ultrasecret folder containing the Project *Wachter* plans was gone.

He ran back into the corridor and slammed into Koppfman, just entering the room.

Both men snarled, then instinctively grabbed at the doorjamb as the ground shook beneath their feet. But the distant blast of Marco's cave charge was too deep and too far away to be heard.

A full hour had elapsed since the end of the attack, and now the other German combat unit commanders, gathered around the map with Meirhausser and Koppfman, heard the steady rumble of truck engines revving up in the courtyard as noncoms shouted for men to board the vehicles.

"They came in from the east, underground," Meirhausser said, pointing to the map. "This old place must have dozens of old tunnels we never dreamed existed. How they got into the tunnel is still a mystery. Whatever route they took when they escaped is now hidden and blocked by the charges they set. But it has to be to the east. I want a triple ring of men out, both to the east and south, just as quickly as you can get there. Colonel Schmidt, coordinate both the Wehrmacht and Waffen assignments. We know they have a German staff car, but judging from the number of guns we heard, they can't all get into that. Every road must be blocked, and that includes back trails."

Meirhausser looked up at the corridor above, and the bile rose in his throat as his gaze paused momentarily at the door to Riva's room. Either she had been taken hostage or, even more outrageous, she had led the partisans to his safe. The truth would be known only when the group was captured.

A senior noncom ran up, followed by a dripping corporal.

"Herr General," he shouted, "begging the general's pardon, sir, but there is something you must know."

Meirhausser raised his eyes to the man. "What is it?"

"A few minutes ago, sir, I called to the rail siding to alert our sentries there. When I got no answer, I sent Corporal Mueller and a squad to check on them. Sergeant Schwitzer and the relief men are dead in the vehicle that took them there. There's no sign of the two men they were supposed to relieve."

Both Koppfman and Meirhausser reacted simultaneously.

The Gestapo officer ran to the command post switchboard at the far end of the hall. "Ring the rail dispatcher's office in Aosta this instant," he ordered.

Across the room, Meirhausser heard Koppfman screaming obscenities into the phone. Koppfman slammed the handset down and ran back.

"They are on a two-car train," he panted as he came up to the group of officers. "They used forged documents to force the rail dispatcher to send the unit up our siding shortly after six tonight. But they have to go north. The rains have washed out the tracks to the south, and they know it. That fool told them."

Both Meirhausser and Koppfman bent to the map. The general's finger traced the rail lines leading out of Aosta. He took one quick look at his watch and then let out a small yelp of satisfaction.

"Schmidt," he called to the Wehrmacht colonel, "what do we have at Alagna?"

"Two full infantry companies, Herr General," the officer replied.

"Any armor?"

"Four armored cars and three Mark Four tanks, five tracked personnel carriers, Herr General."

"Come here quickly," Meirhausser said, "and look closely. If we move very fast, we might just trap them. Here is the rail line, and this is the siding coming from headquarters." The colonel bent close to the map to follow the general's moving finger. "They have to go south from here in order to reach the main line. They probably have reached it by now. There's no way we can intercept them since it runs through the forest with a few cross trails. But look, right here. Here is another siding, just a few miles from Alagna. That means that there has to be a switch on the line."

Meirhausser raised his head and shouted at the Gestapo officer. "Koppfman, get back on the phone with that train dispatcher. Find out if a switch can be set automatically from the Aosta yards. It's the one about eight miles south of Alagna on the main line going north. If so, tell him to throw the switch immediately to shunt that train onto the siding. Wait on the phone until he tells you it's done. Move."

Koppfman ran for the switchboard.

"Schmidt, our commander in Alagna," Meirhausser said. "Give him the coordinates of the end of that siding. Have him load troops, get all armor running, and keep him on the line until Koppfman gets his answer. If we can put that train onto the siding, we've got them."

The Wehrmacht officer ran to a nearby field phone.

Meirhausser looked across the room at Koppfman. The Gestapo officer was holding the headset to his ear, apparently listening. The general drummed his fingers nervously on the map. He could hear Schmidt giving orders to the Alagna commander, forty miles north and east. If they couldn't get to the switch in time, it would be damned difficult to stop the partisans before they reached the Swiss frontier.

Meirhausser studied the map again. The rail line swung northeast around Alagna and skirted through gorges and short tunnels, running along the base of the Matterhorn's foothills before turning north again and diving through a pass into Switzerland. There were no roads in the area, and in most sections, snow remained on the ground year-round. During the soon-to-come winter months, the line was all but abandoned when the passes filled with snow. All he had up there were small patrols of ski troops.

He signaled to another of the waiting officers and gave him additional orders for the ski units to be alerted to the possibility of an escape in their direction.

Suddenly Koppfman held the phone from his ear. "The switch has been thrown," he shouted.

"Schmidt," Meirhausser roared, "get those units moving to the end of that siding, now."

The general quickly folded the map and ran for the door, followed by Koppfman and the other officers.

"Hurry up, damn it," Meirhausser yelled. "I think we can get there before the train does. It's all uphill for them, and we can cut through the forest."

Eight truckloads of German soldiers, led by a half-dozen armored cars, roared out of the castle courtyard and turned north. Meirhausser was riding in the leading six-wheeled armored car, with Koppfman in the second vehicle.

The cars and trucks bucked and churned on the gravel and dirt road, drivers peering intently through the torrential rain, both to keep the vehicle ahead in sight and not to drive off the narrow road.

The general was sitting beside the driver of the first car, electric torch shielded and shining on the map open in his lap.

"Faster, man," he shouted over the roar of the engine, "can't you get more speed out of this thing?"

Despite the cold dampness inside the armored vehicle, sweat streamed from the driver's face as he fought the wheel and put his foot to the floor.

◆　　◆　　◆

It was impossible to make any speed down the winding siding from the castle. Kimball dared not turn on the engine headlight for fear of disclosing their position to German army units that must already be out on search. They crawled downhill in the dark and rain, Cosimo riding the front end of the locomotive with an unlit electric torch in hand. Another of the partisans was at the opposite front side of the engine, and both men squinted into the night for a sign of the switching array that would put them onto the main line.

Both Kimball and Marco had taken advantage of the slow journey to climb back to the freight car, strip off the German uniforms and put on their own clothing. Kimball had just finished dressing when the train lurched and slowed to a halt. He leaped for the open door and peered out.

Cosimo's lighted torch was swinging back in an arc. Led by Kimball, the partisans and Marco jumped from the car and ran to the front of the engine. One man remained in the cab, still holding a gun to the engineer's back.

The Canadian ran up to the big partisan. "Why are we stopping?" he asked.

Cosimo's light played over the rails several yards ahead of the idling locomotive.

"Switch," Cosimo grunted, looking at the tracks that curved back towards Aosta in one direction and down and to the left in the other.

Beside the roadbed was the squat rain-glistening shape of the switching station.

"Automatic switch," Cosimo muttered, as much to

himself as to Kimball. "Those bastards in Aosta have cut us back to the yards."

He studied the rail for another minute and then yelled at his men. "Get the pry bars," he called, "and hurry."

Four of them ran back to the car where Joelle and Adriana were leaning out, peering into the dark.

Three of the partisans jammed bars into the rails to bolster Cosimo's seemingly endless strength. Slowly, the rail moved, opening the way for the train to slip past the switch and away from Aosta. But the moment they eased up on their bars, the automatic mechanism slammed the rail back in the wrong position.

"We will have to hold it open while the train goes through," Cosimo announced. "Eduardo, get in the cab and tell that Fascist bastard to move that thing an inch at a time. Once those great wheels are in the opening, it will hold the switch until the engine passes. Then we'll have to hold it open again for the car."

In the cab, Ed quickly gave instructions to the engineer.

"One mistake, just one little error"—he put his knife just below the man's ear and let the point prick the skin—"and you are dead. Don't think we can't operate this thing without you. Now, move this engine as I said."

Cold fear turned the Italian's stomach to acid. He reached for the braking bar and eased it gently forward like a lover slowly sliding into his woman. The incline was enough to move the train without resorting to steam. The locomotive groaned and shrieked against the brake drums as it inched down the rails.

When the front trucks were two feet away and coming, Cosimo shouted.

The four partisans put their backs to the bar and leaned away from the massive wheels brushing against their legs and feet. The trucks moved into the open switch, and then the front driving wheels.

In a single motion, the four men snatched their bars from the switch before the wheels crushed them. It took a full three minutes for the locomotive to clear the switch.

"Again," Cosimo yelled, reaching with his bar.

Once more, the spring-loaded switch creaked open as the smaller wheels of the freight car tracked behind the engine. Straining and pulling, the four partisans held the rail open until the freight car had passed. Then Cosimo dropped his bar and signaled with his light. The train halted.

"Get into the car," he ordered the other three, "and take the bars with you. We will have to do this again in a few minutes when we get to the main line. As soon as we stop, come with the bars."

He ran for the front of the engine, and, moments later, the two-car train again moved slowly in the dark, its two lookouts posted at the front. Five minutes later, they were at the second switching array, one that could turn a train right to the south or curve it left and north towards Switzerland.

The pry-bar operation was repeated.

Ten minutes later, the Proserpine train was on the main line, heading north. Rain continued to fall, but not as heavily as earlier.

On the floor of the cab behind the engineer, Kimball, Marco and Cosimo bounced and rolled as they crouched over the map that the Canadian had opened.

The train was rocking and slipping on the wet rails as it drove through the thick forest. But without a light to spot barriers, washed-out track or fallen trees, the speed was under twenty miles an hour.

"We've used up too much time," Kimball said. "We're not making speed now. The Germans aren't stupid. By this time they've found the guards at the siding, and have checked and know we've got the train. And we have to be going north because they know the tracks to the south are still washed out. Let's see where we can expect trouble." The trio bent over the map.

148

Kimball studied the rail route. He rocked back on his heels and stared out into the black night for several minutes. A faint smile appeared at the corners of his mouth.

"Marco," he said, "I've got an idea."

He picked up the map and went over to the engineer's side. His light played on the map as he conferred with the man.

The train labored up a long grade and then entered a cut in the mountains. On the far side of the cut, the tracks sloped down to Alagna before again reaching up to the foothills of the Alps. The gorge fell away on both sides to thick forest.

Four miles down the slope, Kimball tapped the engineer on the back. The man nodded and reached for the brake lever. Sliding and protesting, sparks flying from locked wheels even in the rain, the two-car train came to a halt. Kimball remained with the engineer in the cab as the others jumped down and ran back in the rain to the freight car. Ten minutes later, Marco went past the cab to the front of the engine. Another ten minutes went by before he came to the foot of the steps. He looked up at Kimball and nodded.

The Canadian prodded the engineer. "You know where you are, and you've got a long wet walk ahead of you," he said. He pointed out to the right and ahead of the train. "If you don't lose your direction, keep going through the trees. You should make it into Alagna by midmorning. Now, go."

The Italian glared at him angrily, then reached for his coat hanging at the side of the cab. Wordlessly, he swung down onto the steps and then vanished into the night.

Kimball walked to the opposite side of the cab and looked back.

Cosimo was standing alone beside the freight car. When he saw the Canadian's head, he gave a thumbs-up gesture.

Kimball pulled back into the cab and looked around. The firebox door was glowing red, and high-pressure steam vented through a bypass, whistling in the night. Slowly, he eased the throttle forward with his left hand, his right hand wrapped around the brake bar. Steam shrilled to a painful sound as the engine fought against the brakes.

He threw one quick look to the left side of the cab. Then, with a lunging motion, he pushed the throttle full open against its stop and released the brake bar. The old engine seemed to leap forward down the grade.

Kimball hurled himself to the open door and scrambled down the steps. The locomotive was already gaining speed. The Proserpine leader swung out, faced to the front and jumped into the dark. He hit and rolled over and over, gravel and twigs cutting his face and ripping open one pants leg at the knee. Steam streaming from vent and loose connections, the train vanished down the gentle slope.

He was just rolling over to pick himself up when Cosimo loomed out of the darkness; his big hands lifted Kimball to his feet.

Both men were grinning.

"Let's go," Ed said.

General Wilhelm Meirhausser stood in the armored car and squinted through the gun slot at the side. The vehicle was parked thirty feet to the right and beyond the rail barrier and bar that marked the end of the siding. Fanned out in the small clearing were six other armored cars and a pair of Mark Four tanks. Tank cannon and automatic weapons were trained on the end of the rail. In the darkness out of sight, along both sides of the rails, more than a hundred German troopers waited, their weapons at the ready. Behind the general's car, along the muddy road to Alagna, troop-carrying trucks and additional armored vehicles were parked in the dark. More infantrymen stood in the rain beside their trucks, waiting for orders to move if the partisan group should somehow manage to escape the inner net.

The railhead was five miles from the main line. Before

the war, it had been used by loggers to haul timber they dragged from the surrounding forest. But the tracks were rusty and unused, and a train had not traveled the siding in four years. Brush grew between the tracks and along the roadbed.

Meirhausser noted with satisfaction that the rain had finally stopped. If the clouds were moving away, even in the dark, there would be better light. But he had come prepared. On both sides of the siding and just beyond the barrier, three great antiaircraft searchlights were trained on the rails, their trailer-mounted generators coughing in the dark and men standing with their hands on switches to bathe the entire area in glaring light.

The siding was just under four miles from the main line. The general peered at the luminous dial of his watch; in the armored car opposite him, Koppfman was also checking the time.

One of the waiting soldiers, with some knowledge of trains, moved out of the dark and knelt beside the tracks, his ear to the rails.

Suddenly he rose and shouted, "Train coming."

A noncom's whistle shrilled in the night, and men came upright and tense over their weapons. Only the dripping of the rain-soaked trees broke the silence.

Now, those outside the armored vehicles could hear the distant rumble of the approaching train. They strained into the darkness for the first glimpse of the headlamp that would be burning at the front of the engine and which would pick up the white-barred barrier marking rail's end.

The rumbling grew louder with each passing second and swelled to a low roar.

The soldier who had listened to the rail and called out the warning frowned. "He is coming fast, Max," he said to the companion at his side. Both men gripped their rifles tighter. "He should be slowing down now. He's got to know where he is, that he's on the siding." He looked down the straight track, hoping to see the glow of the headlamp as it came around the curve a mile away. But there was only darkness and the thundering crescendo of the oncoming train.

Around the curve and onto the final stretch of track, the empty train roared out of the night, virtually unseen in the darkness, only the reddish glow of its firebox to mark its speeding passage.

It was the same soldier, now thoroughly alarmed, who caught the faint darkened outline of the engine as it raced down the final hundred yards.

"Max," he screamed, "he isn't going to stop. Get out of here, Max, get back." The soldier jumped from the side of the track and raced into the woods behind him, ignoring the harsh shouted command of his sergeant. His companion was at his heels.

The locomotive was traveling in excess of sixty miles an hour when its explosive-laden front end smashed through the barrier. Sheer momentum carried the bulk of the massive engine through the barrier and crushed two armored cars even as its charge exploded. An instant after the blast, the boiler blew up with an even greater roar. Hundreds of pieces of shattered metal cut down men and knifed through thin armor. The great wheels, freed of the bulk of the engine, careened another hundred yards down the muddy road, mangling men and parked trucks before they stopped.

All three searchlights had been shattered in the initial explosion of the charges that Marco had fixed to the front of the locomotive with an impact fuse attached.

But there was light, the bright reddish-orange flickering of flames illuminating the entire railhead clearing as trucks, armored cars and gasoline burned in the night. Screams came both from the men exposed beside the tracks and from the crew of a burning Mark Four tank, on its side and under the huge twisted iron shape of the locomotive's cab.

Meirhausser lay stunned and deafened in his overturned armored car, but otherwise unhurt. A soldier planted a hobnail boot in his stomach as he scrambled to find the rear escape door of the vehicle. The car was lying on its side where the force of the double explosion had hurled it. Hands clawed frantically in the dark, and then the eerie glow of dancing flames lit the interior of the vehicle as one of the double doors fell outward. Meirhausser groped for his cap, then crawled and stumbled towards the open door. Across the wreckage-strewn area, the car in which Koppfman had been riding was also on its side; the Gestapo major was duplicating the general's stumbling attempt to reach the rear door.

The fact that both cars had been parked to the side of the rails and ahead of the barrier had saved them from more serious damage. Of the vehicles to the front of the exploding train, only crushed metal and bloody chunks of human flesh remained to be consumed in the flames of burning gasoline.

Meirhausser got to his feet and slowly pulled his cap to his head. His ringing ears registered the cries of the wounded and trapped. Fire and wreckage were everywhere, and the unwounded were daring death, trying to reach their trapped and burning comrades. In that last terrible minute, listening to the train roar down the tracks unchecked, Meirhausser knew then that the partisans were not aboard, that they had outplayed his gambit. He shook his head and ran in the dark back to the parked trucks where other radios might still be working.

They had sprung the gambit, but he was damned if this was to be checkmate.

He slogged past smashed trucks and dying men who had been caught by the engine's wheels as they hurtled out of the dark. Only the first few vehicles were damaged. Stretching back for more than a quarter of a mile, other troops and trucks stood at the side of the road, the men looking towards the flames, wondering what had happened.

The blocky bulk of a large, wooden-sided communications vehicle caught his eye, and he crossed the road to pound on the rear door.

Even as it opened for him, Major Koppfman came running up in the dark.

Inside the vehicle, with the doors again shut and the bright lights from the towed generator burning overhead, Meirhausser shoved one of the men from a side desk and spread his map on the surface. He turned and barked to one of the radiomen, "Find Colonel Schmidt and any other senior officers and have them report here to me immediately."

"*Zu befehl,* Herr General." The man seized his pot helmet and ran into the dark.

Koppfman was bent low, reading the smallest signs on the map. He straightened and pointed to a spot.

"They had to have stopped and gotten off somewhere in here, Herr General," he said. "You can see by the contour lines that the rails rise to this point, come over this ridge and then drop downhill the entire distance to Alagna. And the siding also slopes away. In order to be certain that the train would keep going, even gain speed, they had to have abandoned it on this down slope."

"You're probably right," Meirhausser agreed, eyeing the map. "If so, they are now on foot, and I intend to make them pay very slowly and very painfully for what they have done. For once, Koppfman, it will give me great pleasure to watch your interrogation."

They were interrupted by the arrival of the first of the senior surviving officers.

Meirhausser began issuing orders. "I want all of your effectives loaded immediately," he barked. "Leave just enough vehicles to take care of the wounded. Leave the dead. We can come back for them. Right now, I want those partisans. Schmidt, get on the radio and contact all units in the Damodossola area. Get them moving south. These bastards are heading for the Swiss border, but we can move faster than they can on foot. I think we'll find them here in the upper tree line, before they hit the snow. But just to be on the safe side, increase all ski patrols. Now, get your men loaded up and these vehicles turned around. We can still catch them if we move."

Schmidt went to one of the radio operators as the others who had crowded into the van pushed to the door.

"And I don't give a damn about air raids tonight," Meirhausser yelled after them. "Turn on the headlights. Speed is more important than security.

"Koppfman," the general said, "get out there and find us a couple of vehicles we can use. And I don't mean trucks."

Meirhausser waited until Schmidt had completed his radio contact and confirmed that two full regiments with supporting armor and other vehicles would be moving south to form a net to join up with Meirhausser's forces. Then, wearily, the Alpengruppe commander climbed down from the radio van and stood in the growing light of the dawn. Flames were dying down around the railhead, and in the gloom, trucks loaded with troops backed and turned in the narrow road, their muddy headlights gleaming in the semi-darkness.

Meirhausser turned and looked north to where the majestic snow-crowned peak of the Matterhorn and Mount Rose were still hidden behind the trees and rising foothills.

Riva, Riva, how could you have done this to me?

The distinctive growl of an armored car came out of the darkness and stopped beside him. Another followed. From the side door of the second car, Koppfman waved and pointed to the lead vehicle. The general climbed in, and the driver slowly picked his way through the infantry trucks to the head of the column.

The sun was up over the mountaintops as the long muddy convoy roared through Alagna and raced northwest towards the forests below the Matterhorn's wide snowfield.

◆ ◆ ◆

They were deep into the trees, moving slowly upward when the distant echoes of the explosions reached them. Again Cosimo led the small file, with four of his men fanned ahead as scouts. Kimball followed the big man, and behind him came Adriana and Marco, with Joelle back of Marco and the remaining three partisans bringing up the rear. Marco and Kimball, along with two of the partisans, carried backpacks containing their remaining equipment and ammunition. What was left of the American's nitrostarch was on his back, and he defied safety rules by carrying the detonators in a side pocket and the fuse wound around his chest under his jacket.

When the faint distant reverberations of the explosions reached them, Cosimo stopped. They listened, but no other sound came to them from that distance.

Cosimo smiled at Kimball. "Sounds like it worked, Eduardo."

Kimball looked in the direction of the rumblings. "Let's hope it was nothing trivial," he said.

Gradually, the Proserpine group moved up through the mountains towards the Swiss border. There were many hard miles yet to go when the first light of day filtered down through the trees.

They stopped an hour later for a brief rest and food. Despite the sun in an unusually cloudless sky, a cold wind was waving the treetops and gusting around the small group. They huddled deeper into their jackets, knowing that the chill was coming to them from the snowfields above, snowfields that had to be crossed to reach safety.

Cosimo was on his feet and the others just rising when one of the men out on the point came hurrying back through the trees.

Kimball was at Cosimo's side when the man reached them.

"Germans," the Italian snapped hurriedly. "Lots of them. There's a road up above, about a mile and a half, running across our front. I thought I heard trucks, so I worked my way up and found a spot where I could watch the road. Then they came. I counted six armored cars, several German jeeps and more than twenty trucks, each loaded with men. When they were out of sight, maybe another mile, I could hear them stopping. And I think there were more behind them."

Kimball had his map out, but there were no markings for a road at that altitude.

"It will not be on your map, Eduardo," the huge partisan said. "I know this road and others up here. What Angelo has seen is the old logging road that cuts across the forest to Valpelline. There are others like it all around us, cut by those who take trees for a living. We crossed one in the dark about an hour ago."

Cosimo called to two of his men who had remained with the main party. He conferred briefly with them, and they melted into the thick brush and trees below them, one angling to the east, the other moving downhill on their own back track.

"Vincente," Cosimo ordered, "you and Pietro stay here with the women and the packs. Get out of sight as much as possible. Eduardo and I will go up and have a look at these graycoats. You should be all right here. We are going just to look, not to pick a fight—not yet."

Of the three women, Riva, least conditioned for the physical exertions of the night and day, sank gratefully back to the pine needles. Kimball and Cosimo moved uphill, while Marco and Pietro piled dead boughs over the packs and put the women into relatively safe hiding places at the base of the trees.

Angelo led the way back up the side of the mountain,

moving quickly and drifting like a wraith from brush to tree, disappearing at times as he blended into the cover.

Fifteen minutes later, the wind sweeping down from the slopes above carried the faint sounds of voices. Now the three men moved more cautiously, heads constantly turning for the sight of any moving object in the trees, ears attuned to all sounds.

A sharp rise loomed ahead, sparse with trees but still heavy with underbrush. Angelo went to his belly, and the others followed suit.

The sounds of vehicle engines were clear off to the right. From the left came the sounds of voices. Angelo and the other two men snaked their way to the top of the rise and under the overhang of a massive boulder. Slowly and gently, Angelo parted the bushes and opened a gap that looked out on the single-lane dirt track running across their front. Two minutes later, a VW jeep and an armored car rolled slowly past the trio, moving from right to left. A dozen other vehicles passed them in the next ten minutes, some going in the other direction.

Cosimo touched both of his companions lightly on the legs and wiggled back down away from the road. When they were back in the cover of the heavier timber, they rose to a crouch and quickly returned to where the others waited. A half mile from the road, Cosimo again gave the strange warbling whistle Kimball had heard several days earlier as they were moving down towards Aosta.

By the time they returned to where Marco, Pietro and the women were dug in, the other three scouting partisans came drifting out of the trees. Minutes later, the two Cosimo had sent downhill arrived.

Roberto, who had backtracked them straight downhill, spoke. "They are across the track we passed in the night, Cosimo," he said. "I could both hear and catch sight of them as they moved along the trail. All on foot, graybacks."

"And there are others to the east of us," the other man reported, "but still far away. There is a big rock sitting on the side of the mountain. I crawled to the top and could look down over much of the valley and all of the slope."

"They know we're in here," Marco growled, "and they're spreading a net. We'd better dig in deeper here and get ready for a fight."

Kimball called Riva to his side.

"You know probably better than we, little one," he said, carefully avoiding any reference to her personal contact with Meirhausser, "what German troop dispositions are from what you may have overheard. Did Meirhausser have enough men at the castle to put this kind of a ring around us?"

She shook her head. "The ones below us are perhaps his own troops," she replied, "but there are strong German garrisons in Damodossola, north of here. Those up there"— she nodded her head upslope—"are probably from there, called by radio."

Kimball let his gaze move slowly around the sloping forest floor on all sides of them. "A lousy place to make a stand," he commented bitterly.

"I agree," Cosimo said, pushing pine needles aside to bare a section of the dirt beneath, "and we will not fight here. When Cosimo fights, it is where Cosimo wants to fight, and this is not the place." He was etching lines in the dirt with a twig as he spoke.

"Pay attention to this, Eduardo." The twig gouged a line running east and west. "This is the road above us. And this is the trail below. Now over here"—the twig moved along the upper gouge to the east—"is yet another road, very narrow, long unused. Where it joins the road that we have just seen, it is probably unnoticed because of the brush that has grown up these past four or five years. But I know it is there. It leads down and then swings east as if going to

159

Alagna, but several miles on it comes out near this lower road." Cosimo jammed the twig into the earth. "And this is where we will fight."

Ed eyed the rough sketch. "It's back downhill and miles from where we are now. If we make a stand there, even if we win, we'll have all this distance to come back up to make it to the border." He sighed and rocked back on his heels. "But you know this country, Cosimo. If that's where we fight, then we'd better get moving."

"No, Eduardo, you don't understand," Cosimo rumbled. "That is where Cosimo fights, not you."

His partisans stirred uneasily.

"There is something the Germans don't know," Cosimo said. "They still don't know how many of us there are. They know that the lovely signorina"—he nodded at Riva—"is with us and that there must be at least four or five others, but they have never seen us in the open or in the castle to make any kind of count. Now, this is what I propose."

He outlined his plan, and when he had finished, Kimball disagreed vehemently.

"You'd be walking right into a trap, Cosimo," he protested. "I won't have it. There has to be another way."

"Eduardo, Eduardo," Cosimo smiled gently, "you always fail to understand Cosimo. There can be no traps when Cosimo moves. These are my mountains, mine and my friends', here. We can move where we want and kill Germans where we want. No, it will be this way. I have decided."

Kimball continued to argue until the big man got to his feet, his scarred face scowling in anger.

"I said that this is no longer a matter to be talked about. Now, if you are going to help, good, shut up and come along. If you do not want to help, then stay here." He turned to his own men. "*Avanti,*" he ordered them. The seven partisans got to their feet.

Kimball glared across at Marco, who shrugged and

went to get the packs. He shouldered his own and moved over to the partisans.

Angrily, Kimball went for his own pack, and the women followed. With a three-man point out ahead, Cosimo led the little column up the slopes to the east in the direction of the hidden and little-used trail.

Climbing wearily on the heels of Adriana, Riva di Savoldi felt the parameters of her mind constricting to the point where she was enmeshed in an ambivalence of emotions about herself and the lean tired-eyed Canadian who had once again changed the course of her life.

She smiled inwardly at the imagery of Kimball, cast in the role of the daring knight rescuing the maiden from the ogre of the castle.

While it might have storybook aspects, a maiden she was not. Nor had she been one, in the virginal sense, when she had first met Eduardo eight years before on the slopes of Saint Moritz. Yet, while she had not been sexually innocent, she had fantasized even then that the gentle and tender physical and emotional love he had shown her was that of a first lover accepting the precious offering of her virginity.

Riva could barely conjure up an indistinct image of the distant cousin who had first seduced her when she was fifteen. Or was it she who had seduced him?

Putting one foot in front of the other in a steady unthinking climb through the forest, she let her eyes rest briefly on Kimball's back, hunched under his heavy pack, moving steadily up in the wake of Cosimo. Despite her physical weariness, Riva felt a surge of desire and longing. Ah, Eduardo, it was you who first made me feel like a true woman, rich in body and emotion. What do you think of me now, Eduardo? Or do you even think of me?

There hadn't been time for even a brief moment alone

since he had burst into her room in the castle. Not a second together that she needed to evaluate the man who had been her lover and who had become a dear friend of the man she later married.

And the man who knew that she had given her body, if not her mind, to a German officer.

While she had nothing to substantiate her belief, she had never doubted that Kimball had bedded with many women since they had parted eight years before after a wild and wonderful month of lovemaking. Men need women, even as women need men.

Riva felt no jealousy about those who had given and received physical pleasure and enjoyment from him. But did he understand that the casual groping and gasping so needed for relief of the body burned as strongly in her as it did in him?

She had surprised herself two years earlier after she had seduced Willi Meirhausser. Riva had been raised in the rigid Italian Catholic tradition, which for centuries had stretched morality and religion to mean that one must feel guilty about so-called adulterous sex and confess to the sin—before again clutching and climaxing. But Riva had felt no sense of wrongdoing in exchanging sex for information with the German.

Yet earlier, even as she had honestly and openly loved the kind and good man she had married, she had found herself in the confessional more than once in self-flagellating admissions that it had been Eduardo, not Milo, who she fantasized was taking her, even as she felt her husband within her body.

Riva had deliberately called up Kimball's physical and emotional presence to blot out the reality of Meirhausser's lovemaking.

Lying beside the handsome Prussian, smoking in the dark and enjoying the feeling of physical relief he had given

162

her, Riva had made Meirhausser a half-truthful answer to his question.

It was the third time she had come to his bed.

"I find it difficult to understand why a beautiful and sensuous Italian woman warms the bed of a German officer," he had said. "That is not to say that I am not both flattered and delighted," he had added hastily.

Riva had smiled in the dark and stretched langorously, enjoying the satisfaction he had given her and knowing she would want him again. How easily men dropped their guard with their pants.

She had leaned over on one elbow and smiled at Willi. "This beautiful and sensual Italian woman warms your bed, Herr General," she said half-mockingly and half in truth, "because she thinks you are a magnificent-looking specimen of manhood who makes her body tingle at the sight of you. At the risk of shocking your gentlemanly manners, my dear Willi, there is the making of a whore in every woman. I wanted you to fuck me."

Meirhausser had chuckled and pulled her to his body.

After that night, he had had no reservation about her presence anywhere within the castle. He had quickly found that her mind and wit were as stimulating as her body. At the end of the first year, there was little that Meirhausser knew or did that he had not confided to his Italian mistress. All that he divulged was channeled south via partisan radio and messenger to British Intelligence.

From the instant she learned that Kimball had been identified as one of the enemy agents who had dropped out of the night near Aosta, Riva di Savoldi had retreated into a nebulous fairy-tale dreamworld, knowing that he would come for her, but never allowing her mind to probe the realities of what might lie beyond his arrival.

Struggling up the mountainside, two lifetimes behind

her and an uncertain future ahead, the dreamworld was gone, but Eduardo remained.

Now she faced the growing realization that she had always loved the Canadian. But had he ever loved her? Or had he come simply to obtain the secret plans and was bringing her along out of necessity, rather than emotion?

Please, Eduardo, she pleaded silently, her eyes fixed on Kimball's back, know that my heart and mind have always been yours. Only you ever possessed me. The others, even dear Milo, merely used me.

Have mercy on me, oh God, she prayed, show me Your forgiveness through him. Mary, Beloved Mother of Christ, have mercy on me.

A dozen yards ahead, Kimball shifted his pack and turned to look back down the line. His eyes caught Riva's, and his face lighted with his smile. He held her in his gaze for a brief moment, still smiling at her, then pushed up the slope after Cosimo.

Riva trembled at his glance, and her legs felt weak at the surge of warmth that flooded her. Thank you, sweet Christ.

Meirhausser's armored car came to a halt at the intersection of trails several miles west of Alagna. The sun was well up in the sky as he walked back down the line of vehicles to the radio van. Koppfman, in the car behind the general, climbed out and followed Meirhausser.

The Alpengruppe commander spent ten minutes on the radio with the commander of the northern forces, already moving south. When he was satisfied with the plans for a coordinated sweep through the forest above them, he climbed out of the van and sent a runner down the line for all combat commanders to report to him.

Minutes later, he was surrounded by a small crowd of both Wehrmacht and Waffen SS officers, with Koppfman representing his own forty-man Gestapo unit.

The map of the area was pinned to the wooden sides of the radio van.

"Schwaben and Bayerisch Regiments," he began, "are now moving out along the edge of this snowfield to fan out across the upper edge. I have been informed that there is an adequate forest road for them to travel west, just below the edge of the tree line.

"They will dismount and move south on foot through the forest. Their vehicles will be stationed at strategic places along this road"—he indicated the map—"to prevent the partisans from slipping through the net and crossing the road to the north. We will move along this southern road below them and then send our men up the hill. Here on the east are the river and the main road from Alagna to the north. I would estimate that they are somewhere within this small area, so that a four- or five-mile line will effectively cut them off. I want two companies and four cars on the main highway and along the river, just in case they try to slip eastward. All remaining troops move out on foot from the south road and up into the trees.

"A forest is a poor place for a rifleman, but we have little choice. Issue all Schmeisser machine pistols and light machine guns that can be hand-carried. They're better for this kind of terrain. Exercise extreme caution when you feel that you may be close to our regiments coming down from the north. Those men have been ordered to identify themselves by shouting their regimental names, Schwaben and Bayerisch. Instruct your people to use the word Alpengruppe to identify our troops. There have been enough good German soldiers killed this morning. I don't want any killing each other. Any questions?"

No one spoke.

"All right, move out."

There was a roaring chorus in unison.

"*Zu befehl,* Herr General. Heil Hitler.*"*

The officers broke and ran to their units. Koppfman remained with Meirhausser. He pulled out a pack of American cigarettes and offered one to the general. Meirhausser took it as he eyed the hatchet-faced Gestapo officer. "Fraternizing with the enemy, Koppfman?" "Spoils of war," the major replied laconically. "You really think we are going to catch them up there?"

"I have no doubt of it," Meirhausser said. "They can't be a large group, maybe five or six. They're on foot and further hampered by towing the woman along with them. No, this time we have them."

"The woman was bad judgment on your part, General," Koppfman said sarcastically. "I think Berlin will be unhappy to learn of your association with her."

Meirhausser snatched the cigarette from his mouth and ground it angrily under his boot heel. "And you're just the one to inform Berlin of the fact, aren't you, Koppfman? Don't be so hasty with your judgments, Gestapo. You all are alike, making instant decisions on a person's guilt. Did it ever occur to you that she may have been taken hostage, that the partisans are using her for a shield or even for trading if they are trapped? Hold your mouth, Major, until we have them and learn the truth."

The general turned angrily away and walked to his armored car. Koppfman was unruffled by the exchange. He smoked calmly and watched Meirhausser's ramrod-stiff back going to the head of the column. Then he turned and went to his own car.

Meirhausser gave his unit commanders fifteen minutes to instruct their men, then the Alpengruppe commander walked to the far side of the dirt road where he could be seen by the greatest number of vehicle drivers. He waved his arm in a circle over his head and pointed sharply to the front. A muffled roar of starting engines reverberated through the forest as Meirhausser climbed into the armored car and rolled west along the track.

The net was forming, and Meirhausser would pull the drawstrings until it closed on the small school of fish caught in the middle.

◆　◆　◆

One of Cosimo's scouts came back and spoke briefly with the leader, pointing to the east.

"The old trail is about a half mile in front of us," Cosimo told Kimball. "Now we swing north."

He gave new instructions to the scout who faded into the trees up the slope.

A half mile further and another of the scouts rose out of the brush, finger to lips. Cosimo waved the little column to the ground, and both Kimball and Marco crawled forward.

"The other road is just above us," Cosimo whispered in his basso voice. "There are four Germans on the road, and they may have found the entrance to the old trail."

Quickly, the partisan leader gave orders to his men. Then, waving Kimball, Marco and the woman to stay hidden, he started to lead the way.

His son ran crouched to his side. "I'll go with you, old man."

Cosimo smiled at the American. "There are things you do very well, Vincente. But you are a city boy. This is something for mountain men. Be patient, my son, there will be fighting for you to do very quickly."

He squeezed Marco's shoulder and then waved his men out to the sides and up the hill. Kimball and Marco put themselves and the three women in a small semicircle, facing uphill, bellied down at the base of the trees. Even Joelle had her M-3 cocked and ready on the needles at her head.

Only the sound of the wind came through the trees. It

was close to an hour before Roberto appeared and waved for them to come forward. The five went into a crouch and followed. They found Cosimo concealed in heavy brush at the side of the east-west road. Four of his men, now wearing German army overcoats over their own clothing and with the familiar pot helmets on their heads, stood guard on both sides of the road.

In the distance, they heard more vehicles coming along the road from the east. Roberto raced across the dirt path and sank into the brush on the far side, where his other two companions waited in hiding.

Kimball, Marco and the women gathered around Cosimo.

"Eduardo, you and Vincente get into cover across the old trail, but on this side of the road. You ladies go down a few yards beyond me"—he pointed west—"and keep your heads down. We will wait for a small detachment before we attack. I will give the signal by firing the first shot. Remember that every German in whatever unit we hit must be killed. Try to avoid wrecking the vehicles. I need them to go back downhill. We must be very fast because the sound of our guns will bring other Germans very quickly."

The Canadian intelligence officer and the American sergeant squirmed their way through the brush to the east side of the old trail and then inched forward. Kimball was at the side of a large boulder and Marco at the base of a tree growing at the side of the larger dirt road. The four partisans in their German disguises stood in the road, Thompsons slung from their left shoulders, German Army rifles resting butt-down in the dirt at their sides. They waited.

Kimball could hear the rising sounds of laboring engines as the German vehicles got closer. From the deep rumbles of the engines, it sounded as though they were trucks. He pressed deeper into the brush and watched the slight curve in the road to his right.

The nose of the first truck came around the bend, followed by five others. Fingers touched triggers as the hidden team waited for Cosimo's signal. There were five trucks in the convoy, and as the first passed him, Kimball could see that it was loaded with troops. The vehicles rolled past the four disguised partisans who stared impassively at the German soldiers as each truck passed them.

Cosimo let them go, and Kimball released the deep breath he had been holding in anticipation of gunfire.

A full twenty minutes went by before they again heard the sound of vehicles. A closed VW jeep, followed by a large truck and a smaller weapons carrier, ground around the curve. There was nothing behind them. Kimball heard a hissed command from Cosimo, and he placed the folding stock of the M-3 firmly against his shoulder, cover open. He caught the slight click of Marco's weapon on his right. As the leading VW approached, three of the uniformed partisans casually moved down both sides of the road towards them. The fourth man stepped into the middle of the trail and raised his hand. By the time the VW had halted, the other three partisans on the road were slightly behind the large troop-filled truck. The weapons carrier, with more men and a light machine gun, slowed to a stop in front of Kimball and Marco.

The canvas door of the jeep swung open; a Wehrmacht junior officer stuck his head out and looked at the partisan standing in the middle of the road.

"*Was ist los?*" he asked.

Cosimo's automatic weapons fire replied, smashing the man's head like an overripe melon and stuttering death along the upper part of the jeep. The Proserpine group joined in, their fire ripping into the troops spilling out of the other two vehicles.

Kimball fired one burst, and his gun jammed. Cursing, he rolled behind the rock and pried at the spent casing caught in the ejection mechanism. The air was filled with sounds of the Thompsons and the higher-pitched crack of German rifles as the soldiers rolled under cover of the truck and jeep to return fire.

The driver of the lead jeep had spotted the ragged peasant shoes and tattered pants showing under the partisan's army coat as he stood in the middle of the road.

Almost in the instant that Cosimo fired, the driver dove out of the vehicle and rolled to the side of the road, gun in hand. He fired, and the Italian in the center of the trail spun and fell. Another of the disguised men lay dead beside the truck. The other two ran for the cover of the roadside, only to be cut down by shots from the weapons carrier.

Kimball finally managed to dislodge the jammed casing and, recocking the submachine gun, rolled back to add his fire to that of Marco, who was raking the weapons carrier. All but a half dozen of the Germans lay dead or seriously wounded.

Three of the survivors crouched under the shelter of the overhang where Cosimo lay, out of reach of his fire. One, a corporal, heard the Thompson roaring over his head. He looked down the road to the west and then signaled to the other two. Both were armed with Schmeisser machine pistols. The corporal rose and then raced along the side of the road under the cover of the overhang. If they broke around the far side, they could take Cosimo from the rear.

They were twenty yards down the road when a slight figure in baggy American Army fatigues jumped into the road in front of them, M-3 submachine gun clutched in her hands, spitting fire. Joelle's burst ripped through the corporal, hurling him back against the man at his heels but partially blocking the third man. This last dove desperately to one side and rolled over, machine pistol spitting a hail of lead. The little Frenchwoman was slammed off her feet like a sodden puppet. The German continued to fire, Joelle's torn body jerking in the dirt as each shot registered.

A burst of Thompson fire came from across the road, and the German soldier screamed and began to die as blood pumped from his torn intestines.

Then it was over. Four of Cosimo's partisans sprawled in death along the riddled road. Cosimo had seen Joelle go down and now ran to her body. He took one quick look and then turned back to the vehicles.

"She is gone," he said, breathing heavily. "We must move fast before they get here. Adriana, signorina, come quickly."

One of the surviving partisans was making his way among the thirty-odd German bodies lying in the road or crumbled inside the vehicles. Knife in hand, he moved from one to another. A wounded German soldier screamed as the Italian leaned over him and, in a single swift motion, laid the man's throat open.

"All right, now, move," Cosimo said urgently to Kimball and Marco. He was holding Adriana tightly by the arm. He shoved her into Marco's grip.

"No," she screamed, "no. I stay with you, Papa." She fought to free herself from Marco's grip.

Cosimo leaned forward and kissed her gently on the cheek.

"Go with your brother, little one, and don't worry. We will all be together later."

"Please, Papa, please," the girl burst into tears, "I belong with you. Don't send me away, Papa."

"You must, child. It is best. We will be fine, never fear. Your brother will get you over the frontier, and when this is over, we will join you. Now, go."

Cosimo turned and looked sadly at his three remaining men.

"So, dear friends, we are now an army," he said. "Roberto, you and Angelo take that small truck. Silvestre, you and I go in the jeep. You drive."

171

The three ran to the vehicles, and tugged and pulled dead Germans to the dirt.

Cosimo looked at Kimball. "Get a few hundred yards north into the woods, Eduardo, then wait. Soon you will be out of the trees and into the snow. Cover yourself well, and wait until you hear the Germans moving south. Wait as long as needed to be certain."

Kimball nodded.

The big partisan turned to Marco, still clutching the sobbing Adriana.

"You are a man, my son," he said softly, "and a very good one. I give you a great responsibility. Keep your sister safe and well. See that she grows, and be certain that the man she marries is as good as you."

He paused and stared deeply into Marco's black eyes.

"I am glad you came. You have given purpose to my life."

Marco shoved the girl into Kimball's grip and stepped to his father. He looked up into the scarred face.

Wordlessly, he threw his arms about the massive man and hugged him.

"You are a man, Papa," he cried brokenly. Then he shoved himself away and, seizing Adriana by the arm, slung his pack over his other shoulder and ran into the trees north of the road, tugging the protesting and sobbing girl in his wake.

Silently, Kimball handed Riva one of the backpacks and slipped a third over his own shoulders.

He looked long and silently at Cosimo. "Good-bye, old friend," he said softly.

"Go with God, Eduardo," the partisan replied.

Kimball took Riva by the hand and led her quickly after Marco and his sister.

Cosimo watched them go and then climbed into the VW. Roberto had edged the weapons carrier around the stalled and riddled truck. Cosimo waved his hand downhill, and Silvestre spun the wheel and plowed quickly into the loose brush at the head of the old narrow forest trail. Both vehicles picked up speed, and bounced and twisted as they raced for their meeting with the Germans waiting below.

The surviving members of the team had barely gotten under cover in the brush two hundred yards north of the scene of the firefight when the first German vehicles came roaring from both directions.

From their hiding place, Kimball, Marco and the two women heard the vehicles stop and then the shouting of German commands as troops poured out of trucks and armored vehicles, weapons cocked and peering into the brush on both sides of the road.

Two Wehrmacht officers had walked through the scene of carnage and found the broken brush and tire tracks heading downhill. As they stood there examining the tracks, gunfire echoed from below them. It was the unmistakable sound of American Thompson submachine guns, interspersed with the sharper crack of German rifles. Again there were shouted commands, and the hidden Proserpine team heard the thud of pounding feet as German soldiers ran back to their trucks.

Two miles down the narrow and almost invisible track, Cosimo and Silvestre let go with another long burst of fire into the surrounding trees. Standing in the weapons carrier behind them, the other two partisans rapidly worked bolts on the German Army rifles they had found lying in the vehicle.

Cosimo grinned and then waved for them to move out. Both vehicles again jounced down the track. Behind them, the first of the armored cars turned into the narrow trail and moved down in pursuit. The Wehrmacht officer sitting behind the driver was talking on the car radio with other German units spread along the east-west road.

The first five vehicles to arrive at the site of the ambush

had just entered the downhill track when other German Army units came roaring to the scene. A pair of infantrymen, left as guides, waved the newcomers onto the downhill track. Another short burst of gunfire came from far below, presaging the flight of the partisans.

Kimball held his group under cover for a full two hours after the last vehicle had been heard. Then, waving for Marco to stay put, he crawled in the late afternoon shadows back to where he could see the road. The bodies of the dead had been removed, and the bullet-smashed hulk of the truck had been shoved off the side of the road and tipped over. The guides had been picked up by the last of the vehicles. Only the rustling of the wind-shaken trees could be heard.

He lay, looked and listened for ten minutes, then crawled back to his companions.

"I think we're clear," he told them, reaching for his pack. "We'll work up to the edge of the tree line before it gets dark and wait there until dawn. I don't want to tackle that ice field at night. There are too many crevices and holes."

Marco rose and helped the two women to their feet. All four stopped in frozen silence as the far-distant sound of gunfire and explosions echoed up from deep in the valley below.

The rippling muted noise continued to drift up to them for a full fifteen minutes. Then there was silence.

Adriana moaned and slumped against Marco. "Papa, oh, Papa," she cried softly, tears cutting paths in the dust on her face. "Oh, Vincente, he's gone. I know it. I just know it."

Marco had an arm around her shoulders as he stared over her head in the direction of the distant gunfire. "Don't worry, baby," he crooned, smoothing her hair. "He's not gone. That tough old son of a bitch is too mean to die."

Kimball led them up through the trees towards the snow.

Meirhausser's long column rolled down the lower road. Behind the general's armored car, Koppfman stood in the turret of the second car. The following six vehicles, including a VW reconnaissance car and six truckloads of Waffen SS and Gestapo SA men, were all under Koppfman's orders. The general's car slowed to a stop at the faint markings of the trail leading north through the forest. Meirhausser opened the door to his car and pointed up. Koppfman nodded and dismounted from the armored car. He walked back to the reconnaissance car and climbed in. The driver shifted into four-wheel traction and turned up the overgrown track, the six trucks following. Once they were clear of the main trail, the column closed on Meirhausser and continued traveling west.

A quarter of a mile up the narrow trail, Koppfman ordered a halt and went back down the line of trucks, issuing orders. The men in the trucks began rolling up the canvas coverings at the sides, giving them visibility as well as a field of fire.

In some places, the track was so narrow that the big trucks scraped sides and fenders against bordering trees. The men in the rear of the vehicles cursed and ducked the overhanging limbs that dragged through the open sides of the trucks.

They were still less than a mile from where they had turned onto the trail when the reverberations of gunfire carried down the mountainside from far above them.

"Can't you go any faster?" Koppfman snarled at the driver.

"No, sir, not without hitting a tree or breaking an axle on this thing."

The top had been pulled back, and Koppfman stood up, holding to the windscreen for balance as he listened to the distant sounds of the firefight taking place at the partisans' ambush site. Seated behind him, the two Waffen SS troopers

175

took tighter grips on their weapons and anxiously scanned the dense forest on both sides of the track. The afternoon sun was already casting long shadows through the trees.

The sounds of gunfire ceased. Koppfman remained standing as the convoy ground painfully upwards along the rutted and overgrown trail.

Ten minutes later, more firing was heard, this time closer. Koppfman shot a quick glance over his shoulder to be certain that all six of the trucks were following. The second bursts of fire lasted but two or three minutes, and again, there were only the sounds of Koppfman's trucks and the car laboring along the track.

A mile farther up the trail, Cosimo stopped both his vehicles and ordered the engines turned off. He stood at the side of the VW and listened.

The wind from above carried the unmistakable growls of powerful engines coming downhill. The huge man turned and stood, hand cupped to ear, listening for sounds from below. Again he heard the roar of laboring vehicles. He called his three men to his side.

"They are in front and behind us," he said calmly, "so we hit them before they hit us. Surprise is always as good as a hundred men.

"Fill your pockets with all the ammunition you can carry. Nothing else."

"We found some of the graycoats' potato masher grenades in the weapons carrier," Roberto said quickly.

"Good, get them, and we'll each take a couple. Now, when we start, we go down fast. Roberto, stay back, give yourself enough time and space. As soon as we see the first truck, we jump, understand? The crash should give us enough time to get into the trees towards the river. We've got to pull them after us, but they'll be on foot then, and we know this country."

He looked up at the fading light.

"Soon it will be dark. If any of us make it, scatter into the forest as soon as it is full dark. With God's blessing, we meet sometime tomorrow back at the caves."

Quickly, he embraced each of the three, then with Silvestre climbed back into the VW. Cosimo clung to the sides to keep from being thrown from the racing pitching little car as it sailed over rock and ruts down the trail. Fifty yards behind, the weapons carrier careened after them.

"There," Cosimo yelled as the front end of Koppfman's reconnaissance car came into view less than twenty-five yards down the trail. "Now," Cosimo shouted and hurled himself out of the speeding car. Silvestre slammed his foot to the floor and tumbled out to the left, rolling over and over and slamming into a tree.

The VW hurtled into the front of Koppfman's car with the ear-piercing crash of tortured metal. The driverless weapons carrier sailed past Silvestre to smash into the rear of the crushed VW, causing the gas tank to rupture and explode. The double impact sent Koppfman into the air over the windscreen of his shattered vehicle. He hit shoulder-first on the hood and bounced off the left, just as the weapons carrier struck and the gas tank exploded.

Cosimo had picked himself up and raced across the track into the trees below. He spun to see the VW collide with the upcoming car. There was no mistaking the black-uniformed, gold-braided figure that sailed through the air and glanced off the hood. Either Gestapo or Waffen, both hated and despised. Koppfman's body was still in the air when a short burst from Cosimo's gun slammed it sideways against a tree. The Gestapo major sprawled like a broken doll at the base of the tree, back to the trunk, arms and legs askew. His face, the back of his head and most of his throat had been blown away by the heavy machine-gun slugs.

All six of the trucks stopped before hitting the wreckage in the trail. The soldiers in the truck immediately behind

Koppfman swung their guns out to the sides. Fire rippled the length of the vehicle as Silvestre raced for the trees. The Italian staggered and threw up his arms to fall facedown.

Cosimo saw Silvestre fall and fired a long burst at the truck, hoping to see his comrade move. He waited long seconds as rifle fire probed the trees for him. Silvestre didn't move.

Dozens of Germans poured out of the following trucks and broke to the woods, weapons held high, officers and noncoms shouting orders. Cosimo darted from his cover at the base of a tree and raced in a crouch to another. There was no sign of Roberto and Angelo. Cosimo fired again, seeing black Waffen uniforms crumple and fall. He turned and plunged down the slope, dodging from tree to tree, using every bit of brush and growth for cover.

A hundred yards downhill he spun at a sound and then eased his finger on the trigger as Roberto crashed through the brush.

"Where is Angelo?" Cosimo asked.

"Dead," the other panted. "Broke his neck jumping out."

Behind them, they heard the soldiers spreading out and coming down the slope.

Cosimo jerked his head downhill, and Roberto disappeared into the lengthening shadows. Hidden in the shade of a massive tree, the partisan leader waited, German grenade in hand. He saw black uniforms moving cautiously down towards him. The heavy undergrowth was channeling the half dozen directly in front of him into a small group, moving cautiously with weapons trained on the terrain surrounding them.

They were twenty-five yards away when Cosimo threw the grenade and ran down the hill. Two shots followed him before the grenade burst, felling all six SS troopers. Seconds later to his left, another grenade detonated. Roberto was still alive and fighting. That would slow the bastards. He plunged through a thick stand of timber and slid over the edge of a shallow ravine. In a running crouch, protected by the lip of the cut, Cosimo vanished into the growing dark.

◆　◆　◆

The temperature dropped rapidly during the night, and the two men and two women huddled together for warmth. Kimball had thrown up a windbreak of fallen boughs and brush, but it did nothing to keep out the creeping cold. Sleepless, he lay on his back and watched the stars vanish under a cover of clouds. Riva was in the curve of his arm, her head on his shoulder, deep in exhausted sleep. Adriana was pressed against Riva's back, her head on her brother's shoulder. Marco dozed fitfully.

They had shared the last scraps of food, and there was a single skin of water remaining as Kimball took mental stock of their supplies. Food and water really didn't matter any longer. Either they crossed the snowfield and dropped down over the frontier into Switzerland in the coming day, or they would be dead or captured. He shifted slightly and felt the pressure of the thick Project *Wachter* folder under his jacket and shirt.

Familiar doubts rose in his mind as he tolled off the silent roster of those who lay dead along the lower slopes of the mountain and in the ancient castle.

Rage welled in him at the remembrance of Joelle's torn body lying in the road. Brave, happy and talented, she was gone along with the others. He wondered if her prisoner husband still lived.

Nothing, nothing could be worth that much sacrifice. Holding Riva in his arms, Kimball swore that he would never accept another mission. Let the bastards court-martial him, let them shoot him, he was through.

Exhaustion finally clubbed him into troubled sleep.

It was still two hours to dawn when Marco awoke. Adriana was pressed tightly to his side, one arm thrown over his chest, her head on his shoulder. The wind had died, but the cold seemed more intense. The stars that he had seen when they lay down for the night were gone, and he could feel, rather than see, the thick cloud layer hanging over the mountains. There was dampness in the chill air, presaging the possibility of rain or snow later in the day.

He glanced down at the head of the sleeping girl and then looked over to where Riva lay in Kimball's arms.

Adriana stirred restlessly in his arms and attempted to snuggle closer. Marco's arm pulled her tighter to him, as if to shield her from the cold.

Fragmented thoughts of the past twenty-four hours unreeled like movie film in his head. It all had a sense of unreality about it, as though he had been witness to some high drama, rather than a participant. The forest around them was almost silent; only the slight rustling of the trees in the light breeze played a peaceful out-of-place accompaniment to his mental review of their entry into the castle and the fighting and flight that had followed. He wondered if his father were still alive.

His mind skipped to the day ahead, a day that would see them either safely across the border or dead.

Sketchy, drifting and insubstantial ideas of how he would manage Adriana's future replaced the combat-filled thoughts of the preceding day.

When his mother had died, it had been his aunt and uncle who stoically accepted responsibility for him. But there had never been anything other than a sense of responsibility. They hadn't been harsh with him, no harsher than with their own five kids, Marco's cousins. The children had accepted him as a member of the family without reservation, more readily than their parents. But there had never been love or tenderness. He had been into his early teens and just starting

180

high school when he recognized his need to be on his own, no longer an unwanted but accepted burden on his uncle's family.

Italian kids, growing up during the Depression years in New York's Little Italy, were streetwise and tough by the time they reached puberty, if they were to survive at all. For the orphaned Marco, it was simply the knowledge that he had to fend for himself as soon as possible. He felt no bitterness towards his relatives. They had their own kids to worry about. In his senior year in high school he fell into a night job at the Fulton Fish Market, paying enough for him to move out of the crowded apartment and into a shabby but clean furnished room in a weathered tenement building. He worked at night and went to school by day all that year, hungrily but happily independent.

Marco was responsible only for Marco, and in the year between the end of school and the start of the war he found a better job, as a demolitions man in construction work.

He joined the army shortly after Pearl Harbor and fell readily into the easy camaraderie of the service. What responsibility he was forced to assume was only that of a good soldier, trained to do his job under fire and not jeopardize the lives of his fellow soldiers.

Now, for the first time in his life, he was responsible personally and directly for the life of another person. The tough streetwise New York kid was almost frightened by the need he felt to care for the sister who had suddenly been thrust into his life.

Today they would cross into Switzerland. He knew the Swiss were neutrals in this long war that was tearing Europe into new patterns of geography and humanity. What would the Swiss do? Probably keep them in custody.

Marco wondered if Kimball could muster enough clout for them to stay in Switzerland until the war was over, or possibly arrange for him to head back to the States with

Adriana. He tried to visualize what they would do back in New York, but his mind refused to conjure up long-range concepts.

The clouds were now faintly visible as billowing dark-gray waves, and he realized the sky was beginning to lighten. He eased his arm out from under the sleeping girl and peered at the luminous dial of his watch. It was close to five in the morning. Marco reached over the two sleeping women and touched Kimball lightly on the shoulder. He was surprised and startled by an unconscious need to squeeze the other man's shoulder as a sign of friendship. He touched Kimball and jerked his hand back, realizing that he was starting to respect and trust the lanky Canadian. He snorted aloud in self-derision. That would be the day when he really respected any ass-chewing officer.

Kimball came awake immediately, his free arm reaching for the weapon at his side. He blinked once and looked at Marco for a sign of possible danger. Seeing none, he eased the sleeping Riva from his shoulder and sat up. The Canadian glanced at Marco and waved his head in the direction of the nearby trees. Both men stood carefully to avoid waking the women, then, weapons in hand, walked silently into the trees several yards away.

Automatically, they reached for dirty handkerchiefs and began wiping the beaded dew from their submachine guns. Neither spoke. When he finished, Marco pulled out a half-empty pack of cigarettes and offered one to Kimball.

"Last pack," he said softly as they crouched and shielded the flame of his Zippo from possible detection. They stayed hunkered on their haunches, the glowing tips of the cigarettes hidden in cupped hands.

"I've got almost a full pack," Kimball said. "Enough to get us through the day." He looked over at the American. "Ready to move it?"

Marco nodded.

"Yesterday was tough," Kimball said. "To be honest with you, today may be worse. We've been moving northwest. When we come out of the trees, we have at least ten to fifteen miles of uphill snow and ice to cross to reach a pass at the base of Mount Rose, then we drop down to the frontier. You can bet your last cent that the Germans have increased the ski patrols in the area."

He paused and looked at the low-hanging clouds eddying slowly across the lightening sky.

"There's damned little cover up there," he continued, "and what there is consists only of humps and bumps in the snow and ice. We get a very small break from the clouds, since it will make the light flat and reduce the long-range visibility of ski patrols. But we won't see them either from any distance. You ever ski?"

"On the streets of the East Side?" Marco sneered. "That's for rich guys."

Kimball ignored the sarcasm. "Let me tell you something about light on a snowfield. Without the sun, we get both a little help and a big hindrance. What you'll see when we come out of the trees will appear to be a smooth flat field of snow. Don't let it fool you. It's bumpy, irregular and filled with holes, some hundreds of feet deep. When the sun is shining, it casts shadows over the snow, and you can easily pick out depressions and rises. In this kind of light, everything will look flat and gray. Watch your footing. You could walk over the edge of a crevasse just a couple of feet in front of you without ever seeing it before you fall. So we'll have to move slowly and carefully. I'll lead, we'll put the women in the middle and you'll follow. I'll concentrate on picking a safe path, which means my eyes are going to be down and ahead. You can assume it's safe footing where the women and I have walked. So you keep your eyes on swivels. Even if you're not sure, if you see any black or dark dots in the distance, sound off. If we run into a German ski patrol, they're going to be able to move one helluva lot faster than we can, so we need all the warning we can get. Have you got one of the ropes in your pack?"

Marco nodded.

"Good, I've got the other in mine. Any questions, Vinnie?"

The American rose to his feet, pinching out the butt of his cigarette and grinding the coal with his heel.

"You lead, I look," he said tersely.

They went back and awakened the sleeping women.

Riva sat up and shivered. "*Ai*, Eduardo, I am frozen," she moaned softly.

Kimball smiled down at her. "You'll warm up quickly once we're moving." He reached down, offered his hand and pulled her to her feet.

Adriana was already up. "We go now?" she asked in Italian, looking at her brother. "We go."

"*Momento.*" She turned and took Riva by the hand. "We must go into the trees," she said simply and led the older woman away. When the women had disappeared into the nearby brush, the men took advantage of their absence to empty their own bladders.

Five minutes later, with empty stomachs growling in protest, Kimball led them up through the trees again, shifting the backpack more comfortably on his shoulders and holding his weapon in hand, rather than slung over his arm.

In fifteen minutes, the brush had thinned and then was gone, leaving only a bed of fir needles underfoot and between the less dense growth of timber.

The Canadian trudged upwards and to his left, moving at an angle to the growing light in the east. Now, individual trees were discernible for several yards. Kimball paused and looked at his compass, then shifted to a course almost due west, still climbing in a slow traverse across the slope of the mountain, skirting the upper reaches of the tree line.

Almost without warning, they were in the last stands of timber, and the vast snowfield above them was visible through the trees. Kimball turned and led them straight up the slope to the edge of the snow.

He stopped as the needles underfoot blended into the drifting edges of ice and snow. Behind him, he heard Marco gasp as he caught his first sight of the fearful and awesome rock and crags of the Matterhorn rising out of the snow far above them. Its crest was hidden in the lowering clouds. Closer was the equally breathtaking view of Mount Rose.

Kimball smiled at the New Yorker gaping at the monstrous mountains above them. "Almost everyone has the same reaction the first time they see those rocks," he said.

"Holy Mother of Christ," Marco muttered. "We don't have to go up those things, do we?"

"You can thank God that we don't," the Canadian said with a laugh. He had his map on the ground and laid the compass upon it. "Come here," he ordered the other three.

He shifted map and compass until both were oriented on the great peaks of the Matterhorn and Mount Rose.

"We are right here," he said, indicating a spot on the map at the upper edge of the timberline. "From here we move up and west, skirting the southern base of Mount Rose. That leads us into a low pass across the ridge. On the other side, we have a downhill climb of less than three miles to the Swiss border."

He pointed to Mount Rose and indicated their general route with his arm. "Each of you fix the route in your mind. If we run into a German ski patrol, it's possible we might have to scatter, so know where you're going. If we get into a fight and any of us are hit, the others take the same route. Only one final thing."

He turned and looked squarely at the two women and Marco.

"We have come a long way and left too many good

friends lying behind us, all for one purpose," he said quietly. "Inside my shirt is the folder with the plans that have cost us so much. If I am hurt or killed, you, Marco, must get them and keep going. The same is true for both you and Adriana, Riva."

Riva started to protest, but Kimball quickly silenced her.

"If those plans don't get across the border, all of our friends and we ourselves will be dead without purpose or reason. We owe it to them, each of us, to try and make their sacrifices worth something. Now, enough talking. Vinnie, give each of us a short swig of water. That's all we have until we get over the border."

Silently and somberly, they each drew quickly at the waterskin Marco passed around. Without further talk, Kimball led them out onto the snowfield.

They settled quickly into a dogged and exhausting struggle uphill to the beckoning rise of Mount Rose. Almost from the moment they entered the field, they encountered unseen obstacles in the gray flat light. In places the snow was soft and they sank in, often to knee and hip depths, making every step a muscle-pulling fight to free one leg and pull the other after it. The irregular surface gave no hint of what lay beneath. They dropped into soft spots without warning and with no idea of how far the entrapping snow might reach before they once again found firmer footing. At each of the unfrozen spots, Kimball and Marco had to assist the floundering women. It was draining them of strength, but it was most debilitating on Kimball, who was trying to break trail for them even as he sank into the treacherous footing.

The quartet struggled upwards for an hour. When they reached an area of snow-covered ice, Kimball called a brief halt for precious moments of rest.

The 15,000-foot peak of the Matterhorn was still hidden within the clouds, as were the upper reaches of Mount Rose.

While they would not approach those heights, they were already near the 8,000-foot level and climbing constantly higher into thinner air. The combination of their physical exertions and the rarified atmosphere was devastating.

Although hidden above the clouds, the sun was well up when Ed again ordered them to their feet. It was as light as it would get for the remainder of the day. Plowing through the snow and slipping occasionally on the ice beneath, Marco tried to look in all directions at once for any indications of ski patrols.

The ice underfoot carried them for several hundred yards, and then the Canadian officer dropped through crust once again. This time it was just a few steps, and they were again on ice and rock, climbing up a sharp rise in the snow.

Kimball trudged across the top and broke a path in the foot-deep snow down the other side. The women moved achingly in his footsteps.

Marco labored to the crest and had taken one step down when he shouted at Kimball and pointed off to his right. The Canadian spun and saw the distant dots. The four had dropped to a crouch at Marco's warning. For a moment it looked as if they had gone undetected. Then the eight far-off figures turned in their direction.

"Ski patrol," Kimball called, looking around for any sort of defensive position. Down the long incline before them and to the left, he spotted the vague outline of a gap in a towering ice peak. It was still several hundred yards away, but the German patrol was more than a mile distant, though moving faster on skis than the Proserpine team. Kimball surged and fought his way down through the loose snow and treacherous ice towards the ice passage. It was now clearly in sight and appeared to cut all the way through high crystal cliffs into the snow beyond. Kimball stopped, and the others gathered around him. The approaching ski patrol was hidden below the rise they had just topped.

"Vinnie," Kimball panted. "Get in there and set a short fuse charge. We'll wait here. As soon as we see the Germans coming over the rise, we'll head into the crack as fast as we can. I hope to God it's decent footing. That should pull them in after us. Wait until we get past you and are clearing the far end, then set the fuse and get the hell out of there as fast as you can. I'll be covering you as you come out."

Marco's response was to charge down in a floundering, stumbling run, unslinging the pack from his shoulders as he thrashed through the snow. Kimball and the women watched him vanish into the narrow opening in the ice.

Kimball moved Riva and Adriana downhill in front of him and cocked his submachine gun.

"As soon as you see the first man hit the top of the rise," he ordered, "take off in Vinnie's tracks. I'll be right behind. Don't stop or even look back until you are all the way through and out the other side. As soon as you come out, Riva, you go to your left for a couple of feet and get flat in the snow. Adriana, you do the same thing to the right. Understood?"

Both women nodded.

It took the ski patrol less than six minutes to reach the rise. The leading trooper poled his way to the top, then shouted and jammed his poles under his left arm, reaching for his slung rifle and hunching his body forward to schuss in a free run down the slope.

By the time Kimball had yelled "go," both women were already on their feet and moving as fast as they could in Marco's tracks. In the flat light and the excitement of seeing their quarry so near at hand, the Germans missed Vinnie's footsteps leading to the ice passage.

They were still out of range of the submachine gun as Kimball raced after the women. The leading trooper, knees bent in perfect control, raised his rifle to his shoulder and fired as Adriana ran into the entrance to the left. The whine of the bullet choked off as the slug knocked ice from the side of the wall above her head.

Now Riva was into the opening. Kimball was close at her heels when he turned and fired a short burst in the general direction of the racing skiers.

He didn't score a hit, but the effect was enough to send the first man curving off the trail and slow pursuit momentarily. The Canadian spun back and ran into the narrow opening. The passage immediately swerved sharply to the right. When he turned the corner, Kimball could see the far end of the cut about a hundred feet ahead. Marco was standing two-thirds of the distance down the narrow passage, pressed against the wall, gun in one hand, flaming lighter held inches from a fuse in the other.

"How many?" he yelled as Kimball shot past him.

"Eight," Ed called back as he ran for the far exit and out into the snow beyond.

Marco waited until he heard the sound of skis sliding and chattering on the snow as the leading German trooper checked, bringing his skis together to enter the narrow passage. Then the American put the flame to the fuse. It began sputtering and burning.

Marco dove for the exit, staggering and falling and then picking himself up, racing for the open snow. He came out of the ice passage in a stumbling, staggering run, took two steps and dove to his left in a sprawling facedown fall into soft snow. He clawed and fought at the snow around him, trying desperately to roll over and turn to face the opening, his M-3 grease gun clutched in his left hand.

The German soldier leading the file through the cleft saw Kimball crouched in the snow beyond the far entrance. He took a firm grip on the Schmeisser machine pistol in his hands and came skiing out of the tunnel, gun firing as he emerged. Riding on the heels of his skis, the second trooper was also firing at Kimball as he followed his companion out of the passage. Kimball half-rose as the Germans skied from the opening. He took a short step back to brace himself against the recoil of his weapon. His foot broke through the crust, sending him teetering back, off balance, gun barrel pointed skyward. He was subconsciously aware of the impact of the bullet that slammed into his left thigh and sent him racing back into the snow. His body hit the thin crust, and he was falling backwards and down into a hidden crevasse. He slammed into the bottom of the ice trap at the moment that the chattering of Marco's gun was drowned by the roar of the exploding charge. The ensuing avalanche of snow and great blocks of ice engulfed the six German ski troopers still in the passage. They died at the very moment their two companions in the lead jerked and spun in the snow under Marco's fire.

The sound of the explosion was still echoing and reverberating off the slopes of the ice-covered mountains as Marco and the two women hurried to the spot where Kimball had vanished. The American was closest and saw the gaping hole through which Kimball had fallen. He called a warning to the women, then went down on his stomach and inched up to the lip of the opening. Kimball lay in a motionless crumpled heap twenty feet below. Gun still in hand, Marco rolled over on his back for a quick look at the powdered snow and ice still hanging in the air, marking the place where the ice passage had been. He waited a full minute, gun in hand, for any sign of movement, then, satisfied that none of the Germans had survived, he squirmed back away from the edge of the crevasse.

"Wait here," he snapped at the women and trudged back to retrieve his backpack. He looked over to where the two ski troopers reddened the snow with their blood. Neither moved. Marco picked up the pack and circled to check the pair. Both were dead of head wounds.

As the women watched, he pulled the climbing rope and

two mountaineers' ice axes from his pack.

"Help me," he ordered as he began shoveling snow away from the ice sheeting beneath. The women scooped snow with him to bare the ice in a six-foot-long strip leading away from the crevasse. Marco was already chopping into the crystal-hard surface. In five minutes, he had cut a pair of foot-deep holes in the ice with the flat surface of the holes facing towards the crevasse. Two similar gouges were hacked out six feet back.

He uncoiled the rope.

"Riva, here," he commanded, pointing to the first pair of holes. He spun two coils around her waist and secured them in a knot. "Lie down on your back with your feet wedged against the front of those holes." He belayed more rope about the younger girl. "Lie down and put your feet into the other holes."

Both women were on their backs, feet toward the crevasse, the running length of the line in their hands. Marco drove one of the ice axes into the hard surface behind Adriana's head and took three quick hitches around the blade. The other pick went into the ice in front of Riva's feet with additional hitches.

Marco whipped the running length of the line about his own waist in a rappelling sling.

"I'm going down to get him," he told the women. "You've got to hold me. Keep your backs straight and your knees locked. Try not to let the rope pull you off your back. It won't be so bad going down, but it could be rough when I climb back out."

"Go," Riva panted, taking a death grip on the rope, "don't talk so much."

Again Marco squirmed to the edge of the crevasse. Holding to the rope, he swung his legs around and over the edge. He hesitated a second, then dropped in a virtual free fall, checking himself only slightly an instant before he slammed into the ice on flexed knees beside Kimball's still form.

The Canadian was lying partially on his face and right side. Blood still welled from the bullet wound in his left thigh, congealing in the frigid air. His right leg projected askew under his body.

The American sergeant carefully slit Kimball's left trouser leg enough to expose the damage. The bullet appeared to have passed completely through the muscles and fleshy part of the limb. He poured sulfa powder into the wound and hastily tied a pair of field dressings to both sides of the hole.

While he secured the dressings, he looked anxiously at Kimball's other leg, partly covered by his body.

Gently, he began to turn the Canadian onto his back. Kimball moaned, still unconscious. As Marco rolled Kimball's shoulders back and lifted the bullet-punctured left leg away, he shuddered at the sight of the shattered bone of the right leg, projecting through a rip in the trousers. Kimball was now on his back and still moaning. Marco tried to ease the right leg over, and Kimball came back to consciousness screaming.

Riva's stomach churned as the Canadian's agonized voice echoed out of the hole. She turned her head and vomited onto the ice beside her, never releasing her grip on the rope.

Marco had taken his hands from Kimball's leg, and now the Canadian looked at him with pain-glazed eyes.

"Inside my shirt, he gasped. "The folder. Get it!"

The American leaned over the prostrate man and carefully reached under Kimball's clothing to take the green folder. Marco unzipped his jacket and stuffed the folder under his shirt, behind the waistband of his trousers. Resting on his knees, he untied the rope from his own waist and started to ease it under Kimball.

"No," Kimball croaked, "forget it. Get out of here and get the women over the border. I can't walk. I'd just slow you down."

Marco ignored the injured man, continuing to secure the rope around Kimball's chest.

"Leave me, goddamn it," the wounded man hissed. "Leave me and get out of here . . . and that's an order, Sergeant."

Marco finished lashing Kimball to the rope, then stood up. He looked down at the pain-wretched face of the Canadian.

"Fuck you, Captain," he said calmly. He leaned back and shouted up the hole, "I'm coming up."

Marco tried to ease his weight onto the rope and then inched his way up, hand over hand. Above, the rope cut into the hips and waists of the two straining women, lying with backs arched and feet jammed against the ice holes to take the strain.

Near the top, the American briefly twisted the rope around one leg and reached for the jagged edge of the hole. He pulled himself up by his fingertips until he could jackknife his body over the edge onto the snow. He eased back from the edge and unhitched the front ice axe, quickly cutting himself footholds in the ice.

"OK, now we start pulling," he told Riva and Adriana. "He's hurt badly. When we move him, he's going to scream like a stuck pig. But if we don't get him up, he's going to die there."

He belayed the line around his own waist and, standing with his heels and soles jammed into the ice, slowly began pulling on the line.

Instantly, Kimball started to scream and kept screaming as Marco heaved on the line and the women behind him took up the slack. Both of them were lying with tears pouring from their eyes and quickly freezing on their faces as the

Canadian's shrieks lanced their ears. Then, as if choked off by a hand clapped over his mouth, Kimball was silent.

Marco, muscles corded and straining as he pulled, gave a small sigh of relief. Kimball had lost consciousness. Two minutes later, he was dragging the still form of their leader back through the snow from the crevasse. The shattered right leg lay at an odd angle from his body, broken below the knee.

Marco dropped down beside the still man. "Adriana," he barked at his sister, "get those ski poles from those dead bastards."

Both women were untying themselves from the rope. The young girl dropped the coils and slogged quickly to the side of the German troopers.

Moments later, she lay the four ski poles beside her brother. Riva was at Marco's side, holding the cloth up and away as he cut it from the broken bone. She shuddered in horror as the leg was laid bare, the jagged end of the shinbone projecting from a bloody wound.

"Jesus," Marco said. "I hope to Christ he stays out for a while."

He studied the broken leg, then gently but firmly pulled at Kimball's ankle as Riva put her weight across the unconscious man's lower body for leverage. The shattered end of the bone receded a couple of inches into the wound until its tip was barely visible. Then Marco could pull no more, and Kimball was again moaning.

"That's as far as it will go," Marco said. "We'll have to splint it as tightly as we can in that position, drape a couple of dressings over it and then cover him up. If I pull any more, it could cut an artery or jam into the other end of the bone."

The leg was partially straightened. Working as quickly as he could in the cold, he snapped off all four of the poles and placed the pieces, two on each side of the break, against the leg. He lay the last two surgical dressings in his field packs over the open wound. He stood up and tugged under his jacket until his shirt was free of his waistband. The knife ripped into cloth as, with Riva's help, the entire bottom of the shirt was cut off and split into three strips that went tightly around the leg and splints.

When he was done, he rose and stretched for an instant.

Still on her knees beside the faintly moaning Kimball, Riva looked up anxiously. "But how do we carry him?"

"I've thought about that," Marco said, walking away from her.

He returned, carrying the dead Germans' skis. With sure slashes, he cut the harness straps from both backpacks. The four long wooden Nordic skiis were lashed together through their leather boot bindings, and Marco surveyed the makeshift sled.

"It'll never hold together," he muttered. Again he went back to the dead Germans, returning with the small-caliber machine pistol. He switched the gun to single-round fire, then placed the barrel against the wood at the heels of the two outer skis. He pulled the trigger and prayed the sturdy ashwood wouldn't shatter. A single neat hole pierced the wood. Moments later, there were holes both in the curved tips and in the heels of the outer skis. Marco peeled back the nylon rope until only four strands remained, barely small enough to force through the holes. When he was finished, a length of rope stretched across the tops of the ski heels, secured in a small knot on the underside.

The other sections of the rope were forced through the tips in a long loose five-foot arc.

"Those knots may make tough going, but it's going to be tough any way we look at it."

The still-unconscious man was laid on the makeshift sled, faceup with his head to the front, and Marco lashed him to the bindings.

Marco stooped and rummaged through the mutilated backpacks, stuffing ammunition clips into his pockets and passing others to the two women. He found Kimball's M-3 lying in the snow, where it had fallen from his hands as he went into the crevasse.

"You ever fire one of these, baby?" he looked inquiringly at his sister.

"You forget who I am," she said haughtily, reaching for the weapon. "I am Cosimo's daughter. Of course I have fired the American gun. We had these before Cosimo found the Thompsons."

She unsnapped the long clip cartridge, then lifted the cover and worked the bolt expertly before replacing the clip and slinging the gun over her shoulder.

Marco grinned in approval. "Maybe you and I will go into business robbing banks when we get back to the States," he said. "Make a great headline in the *News.* 'Brother and Sister Hit Chase.' "

Adriana looked puzzled.

"Forget it," Marco said. "Let's get out of here."

He stepped into the loop of rope and leaned his weight against it. The ski sled with Kimball aboard began to move. With the two women at either side of the sled, Marco bulled his way toward the now-visible gap at the base of Mount Rose. It was a backbreaking effort, but once moving, the skis slipped easily across the snow. Only when they were forced up a rise did Kimball's weight necessitate all three hauling on the rope to struggle their way up.

They paused for a breather at the top of the fifth such climb in the past two hours. It was close to noon, but clouds still covered the sun.

"Both of you watch for more ski patrols," Marco cautioned his two charges. "The closer we get to the pass and the border, the more of them we can expect. I can't look around much when I'm pulling. If you see anything, yell."

He moved into the rope again and pushed onward. Two hours later, they were, unbelievably, at the top of the pass. A relatively level floor of snow stretched ahead of them for more than a mile, then vanished from sight. It would be downhill from that point on. But that extended mile virtually brought them to a gasping halt.

Protected on both sides by the rising Alps, the snow that fell in the pass was seldom scoured by the prevailing northerly winds. It just fell and piled ever deeper in drifts. The trio found themselves floundering in waist-deep snow, Riva and Adriana moving ahead of the straining man pulling the sled, forcing their pain-wracked bodies through the snow to make a narrow path for Marco to follow.

Behind the laboring American, Kimball was semiconscious, mixing low moans of pain with unintelligible mutterings.

Three hundred miles to the south, His Majesty's Sixteenth Belvedere Rifles were fifteen miles north of Imola, the regiment's left and western flank right against the mountain ridge that dropped away to the plains and marsh of the Adriatic on the east. In that direction was the thin wet line of the Royal Scot Fusiliers, and anchoring the eastern coastal plains were other divisional and regimental elements of Alexander's British force.

For eleven days the rains had ceased for less than five hours at any time. Straddling the main road to Bologna, the Belvederes were ankle- to knee-deep in sucking clammy mud. The churned road was hardly better. Five of the fourteen medium tanks giving fire support to the infantrymen were sunk to the top of their tracks in a broken line back to Imola. The trucks and recovery vehicles that tried to haul them free were soon trapped in the same muck.

Kesselring's Wehrmacht artillerymen had had four years to establish base-point registration angles for virtually every major crossroad along the shank of Italy. Ignoring the rain and fog, the German eighty-eights had been laying down a constant curtain of fire for the past hour. Again the Belvederes heard the roaring whine, and a lance corporal yelled, "Incoming!" as they flung themselves prone into the rain-filled pools of mud. The shells passed over the mud-sodden men and bracketed the lead tank, which slipped and spewed water and mud as it clawed its way forward.

Two minutes later, four more rounds fell, and two of them pierced the frontal armor of the tank. There was a muffled roar as the racked rounds of ammunition inside the hull exploded, turning the interior of the vehicle into a giant meat grinder.

Five miles west of the Belvederes, GIs of the American Thirty-sixth Division slipped and fell, got up and slid some more across the rocks and rain-slick slope of the mountains, trying to maintain contact with the British on their right and stay close to the enemy dug in ahead. The natural fall line of the mountain channeled men into the base of a V-cut, its arms spreading north at an angle ahead.

A steep rock face forced them into single file, and as the leading GIs scrambled up the incline, scores of others piled into the depression, waiting to tackle the rocks. Six hundred yards above, at the mouth of a narrow cave, a stubble-faced German artillery spotter watched the growing mass of men entering the cut. He reached for his radio.

Two minutes later, five Wehrmacht batteries fired a time-on-target salvo. The gun crews slammed new rounds into the smoking breeches, and a second fifteen rounds roared away. After the third salvo, only the wounded moved in the mountain cut.

Both mortar and howitzer fire was falling to the east, cutting into the slogging line of the Belvederes and the Royal Scots.

Rain fell in blinding sheets as the leading platoon worked through the mud towards the dim and wavering low bulk of a village less than a quarter mile distant. The men were out in the open, dragging one mud-encased foot out of the muck to take another step, when they were caught in the interlocking fields of fire of four heavy German machine guns. The platoon died in the mud. Behind it, other Belvederes went to the slime for protection. Fire chewed up some of them, and four men, wounded by machine-gun fire, drowned in less than four inches of water as they fell face-down in the mud.

A half hour later, the order was passed up by word of mouth.

Choking and cursing in the quagmire, the British infantrymen eased back, each line covering the withdrawal of the one ahead in leapfrog fashion.

Alexander's gambling drive for the Po River and the Alpine passes beyond came to a filthy, mud-caked halt. It was the first of November, 1944, and it would be seven months before Allied forces would muster strength to battle north.

As both Alexander and American commander General Mark Clark pulled their forward units back to dig in for the winter, each wondered if they would be walking into *Festung Bergskrieg,* when they would ultimately drive north to Austria. Only Alexander was aware that at that moment an attempt was being made to purloin the plans for the mountain fortress.

◆   ◆   ◆

That lone stretch of snow took them nearly three hours to cross. At the far end, Riva sprawled forward in exhaustion and felt herself slowly sliding downward. The pass had been conquered. Both Marco and his sister sank down into the snow near Riva, drained and beaten.

It was a full half hour before they were able to regain their feet and a last semblance of strength. Their brief rest in the snow was made even more frustrating by the vista that spread before them.

In the distance were more of the snow-covered Alps.

The snowfield fell below them in a long incline, ending nearly three miles away at the top of the treeline. Beyond the upper line of timber, undulating waves of evergreen stretched out of sight down to the distant valleys. According to Kimball's map, the Swiss border lay a scant hundred yards above the edge of the trees.

Marco forced himself to his feet and moved back into the rope harness. He tugged, and the sled, with the now-hallucinating and feverish Canadian, broke free of the snow and began moving. Marco trudged down the slight slope, and as the sled reached them, Riva and Adriana took up their posts at either side.

But again, in the flat dull light of the late fall afternoon, the appearance of the snow ahead deceived them. Although it dropped towards the trees, it was pocked with depressions and wind ridges and the same thin collapsing crust that jammed them into knee-deep snow. On the sled, Kimball lapsed into occasional moans, but his feverish mutterings ceased.

They worked their way down the slope, fighting the sled up a rise and breaking trail down the lower side.

They topped one rise and started down the other. In his near-exhaustion, Marco never saw the sheet of bare ice until he stepped onto it. His feet slid from beneath him and he fell to his back, skating down the glassy incline. He was still tangled in the rope harness when the sled with Kimball's body rammed into him and rode partially over his chest. Marco clawed and kicked frantically to keep the makeshift sled from skidding sideways and spilling Kimball to the ice.

Marco slid sideways down the ice, his hands fighting at the tips of the skis jammed over his chest. Fifty feet down the slope he was slammed into soft snow, and the sled came to rest atop his exhausted body. It took Riva and Adriana, who had seen the ice and skirted it, to pull Kimball from Marco's prone body and help him back to his feet. Now too weary even to be conscious of his protesting body, he dragged the sled down the slope.

The footing became firmer as they reached sections of hardened crust.

They crossed another level shelf in the snow, and the two women moved without command into the rope to haul the sled up a slight rise ahead of them. They broke across the top—and gasped at the sight of a six-man German ski patrol poling rapidly up the slope towards them, still hundreds of yards below. They had been spotted higher on the slope.

Cursing in both English and Italian, Marco jerked the sled around, and the group slid back down the rise they had just climbed.

"Adriana," he snapped, "get back up there on your belly and watch them. Tell me which way they come."

Wordlessly, his sister clawed her way back up and threw herself into the snow just below the crest. She worked her way forward until she had the patrol in sight.

The American looked quickly in both directions. The ridge ran for three hundred yards across the face of the fall line. They were nearer to the northern end. He leaned over the sled and put his face almost to Kimball's.

"Captain," he said urgently, "can you hear me?" Kimball's eyes opened but appeared to be out of focus. Savagely, Marco slapped the wounded man across the face. "Wake up, Kimball. Listen to me. We're almost there, but there's a Kraut patrol coming in on us. Listen to me, damn it!" He slapped Kimball again, and this time Ed's eyes widened and he nodded his head feebly.

"We've got one chance of getting out of this," Marco snapped, "but you've got to help."

Again Kimball nodded.

"You understand what I'm saying?"

"I hear you," Kimball croaked.

"There's a six-man ski patrol coming up the hill towards

us right now," Marco repeated. "I think there's about one chance in hell of boxing them, but I've got to get you off this sled, and you've got to stay awake to help."

Kimball struggled feebly to sit up. Marco pressed him back.

"Not yet. I'll tell you when. Now, listen."

Adriana called from the top of the rise, "Vincente, they have split into two groups, three in each. I think they are going to try to come around both sides of this hill."

"Get down here fast," Marco said.

The girl slid back a couple of feet, then rose and ran down the now-beaten path. Quickly and urgently, Marco briefed the two women on his plan. Moments later, the three of them were hauling Kimball quickly towards the nearer edge of the rise.

Out of sight below the rise, the slope dropped sharply. The Germans, who had been moving their skis straight up the slope on climbing skins, now were slowed into a tedious herringbone step up the steep incline. The trio on the left was close to the northern edge of the wind ridge that hid the targets from view. On the right, the other three had a long traverse to make before they could round the southern flank. The men in the nearer group kept their eyes on the ridge, ready to drop ski poles and unsling weapons at the first sign of the partisans they had been warned to watch for.

The soldier at the rear shouted and pointed with his pole. Above them and emerging from the protection of the rise, the ski troopers saw the three figures and sled moving painfully back up the side of the mountain. The troopers jammed their poles into the snow and hurried their climb, eyes fixed on the group above them. The slope shallowed just below the end of the ridge, and now they climbed rapidly around the mounded incline of the wind ridge, closing the gap that would put the partisans in easy rifle range.

They poled around the corner and towards the track

made by the slowly rising sled and the three enemies. The lead trooper uttered a short command, and they all dropped their poles to reach for their rifles.

Sprawled in a shallow depression at the base of the ridge behind them, the nearly delirious Kimball rested the barrel of his submachine gun on his left arm. He fought to keep the wavering figures in view.

His finger closed on the open trigger. He swept the gun from left to right, slashing through the backs of the three Germans even as they lifted rifles to shoulders.

A great red cloud rose behind Kimball's eyes; he never saw the skiers fall as he lapsed into unconsciousness.

At the first sound of the gun, Marco and the women whipped around and ran back down their own track, the improvised sled bouncing and sliding behind them.

Kimball lay slumped over the edge of the snow parapet. It took long seconds to haul him out and again lash him to the ski sled.

Marco shot a quick glance over his shoulder to the far end of the ridge. The other three Germans had not yet come in sight.

"Pull," he grunted, and the three put their weight into the rope harness. They moved rapidly past the dead Germans, following the tracks the troopers had made in the snow. Fighting for footing, they rounded the north end of the wind ridge and again faced the downhill slope, with the tree line less than a half mile away.

Marco stopped and slipped out of the rope to break a short trail to the front and lower edge of the ridge. He looked to the south in time to see the last man of the second German trio hurrying around the corner, out of sight.

"Now," he shouted, jumping back into the rope. They slipped and skidded down the steep incline, trying to keep the ski sled from overrunning them. Again, the grade shallowed out into a depression with another short rise in front of them.

The women and man fought agonizingly up the incline. At the top, the slope dropped sharply in front of them; there were no further barriers between them and the tree-line base less than a quarter of a mile below.

Marco heard the whine of the bullet before the sharp cracking sound of the rifle reached them. He shoved the women to the snow and peered back over his shoulder. Two of the ski troopers were already speeding down the slope towards them from the upper ridge. The man who had fired poled after them, rifle slung from his shoulder.

The American looked down the steep slope, his eye catching the glinting traces of bare ice reflected in the dull light.

Two of the Germans were less than a hundred yards away and closing fast.

Marco jumped to his feet and pushed the makeshift sled to the edge of the drop.

"On top of Kimball," he yelled at the women, pulling them sprawling across the unconscious form of the injured man. Marco strained and shoved, and the skis began to move. Suddenly the tips dropped downward.

He hurled himself atop the two women, clutching them both in his embrace as the improvised sled tobogganed wildly down the slope, picking up speed as it crossed each patch of ice.

The German ski troopers swept around the short rise and schussed down in rapid pursuit.

Despite the weight of the four bodies, the lashed-up sled bounced and careened off small ice bumps and irregularities, threatening to fly apart in its mad run downhill. Now the sled was moving faster than the pursuing skiers, picking up speed with each second. The line of trees below began to grow larger, and Marco shut his eyes and prayed.

Both women screamed as the wind whipped their faces in the dizzying descent. The lashed-together tips hit a hard short rise of snow and ice.

The sled hurtled off the top of the rise and was airborne when its fear-sickened riders smashed into a massive and deep drift of soft snow less than fifty yards from the nearest tree.

Worn straps snapped and wooden skis splintered as the entire jury-rigged contraption ruptured apart, sending four bodies plunging into the deep snow.

Their noses, mouths and ears were plugged with snow as the stunned women and the American clawed their way out of the snow.

Riva appeared at the moment Marco pushed clear.

"Find Kimball," he shouted and tugged his submachine gun around to cover the women.

He peered up the slope, running a wet sleeve over his eyes to brush away the packed snow. A hundred yards above him, the three German ski troopers had come to a sliding checking stop and now stood, guns pointing down the slope at him.

Warily, Marco waited for the shots to come. There was nothing more he could do. The Germans were out of accurate range of the cheap mass-produced M-3 in his hands. To his right, he heard Adriana's voice blending with Riva's as the two women pushed the snow from the nearly dead Kimball and cleared his mouth and nose.

Marco caught a flicker of movement out of the corner of his eye. His head jerked around to see more than a dozen ski-equipped soldiers closing in from his left. He shot a quick look back to the right to see another large patrol moving in from that direction.

Those on the left were closest as the American brought the stock of his weapon to his shoulder. The clouds broke and the setting sun suddenly dazzled off the glistening reaches of the Matterhorn.

What a hell of a place for a New York street kid to die.

Then he frowned and squinted puzzledly at the approaching ski troopers. In the level snow of the upper treeline, they slip-skied towards him, ski poles on their backs and rifles held waist-high at the ready. But their eyes and weapons were aimed uphill at the three German troopers. Even as Marco watched, the uphill trio slung weapons and poled slowly away to the north.

Emblazoned on the forest-green ski jackets of the approaching soldiers was the crimson shield and white cross of Switzerland.